"Stop, thief!" Shelley shouted as she chased after the tall stranger who'd been shoplifting jewelry from the counter.

He turned back at the sound of her voice, and she threw herself at him like an angry Scottish terrier. Taking up handfuls of trench coat to keep hold of him, she managed to foil his escape. But now that she had him, what was she going to do with him?

"Someone get the manager," she called to the crowd that was gathering. "Quickly."

She looked up into the man's eyes and found them disconcertingly amused. "What took you so long?" he murmured for only her to hear. "I thought I was going to have to come back and do this all over again."

She straightened, releasing one hand but keeping hold of him with the other. Looking up into his sparkling blue eyes, she frowned. "I don't get it," she began. "Do you mean to tell me you *wanted* me—"

"Ssshh." He put a finger to her lips. "I'll explain everything over lunch. . . ."

WHAT ARE *LOVESWEPT* ROMANCES?

They are stories of true romance and touching emotion. We believe those two very important ingredients are constants in our highly sensual and very believable stories in the *LOVESWEPT* line. Our goal is to give you, the reader, stories of consistently high quality that may sometimes make you laugh, sometimes make you cry, but are always fresh and creative and contain many delightful surprises within their pages.

Most romance fans read an enormous number of books. Those they truly love, they keep. Others may be traded with friends and soon forgotten. We hope that each *LOVESWEPT* romance will be a treasure—a "keeper." We will always try to publish

LOVE STORIES YOU'LL NEVER FORGET
BY AUTHORS YOU'LL ALWAYS REMEMBER

The Editors

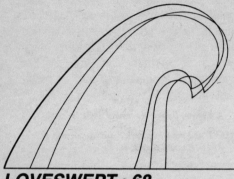

LOVESWEPT · 68

Helen Conrad
Undercover Affair

BANTAM BOOKS
TORONTO · NEW YORK · LONDON · SYDNEY · AUCKLAND

UNDERCOVER AFFAIR

A Bantam Book / November 1984

*LOVESWEPT and the wave device are trademarks of
Bantam Books, Inc.*

ISBN 0-553-21676-7

Published simultaneously in the United States and Canada

---

*Bantam Books are published by Bantam Books, Inc. Its
trademark, consisting of the words "Bantam Books" and the
portrayal of a rooster, is Registered in U.S. Patent and Trademark Office and in other countries. Marca Registrada. Bantam
Books, Inc., 666 Fifth Avenue, New York, New York 10103.*

PRINTED IN THE UNITED STATES OF AMERICA

O   0 9 8 7 6 5 4 3 2 1

To Marie R.–F.,
with love, admiration,
and love.

One

Shelley Pride stared at the shiny gold chains that swayed on the department store display rack in front of her. The handsome man in the unseasonable trench coat had just picked up a very expensive watch and dropped it into his pocket. She'd seen him do it. And when her dark eyes, wide with shock, met his across the long glass counter, he winked at her.

She pushed back a heavy curtain of blond hair and looked nervously around the store. What was she going to do about it? Her fingers clenched into fists, and she gazed down at the scarlet nails, not really seeing them at all.

She couldn't let him get away with it. He was shoplifting. He was stealing, not only from the department store, but from every other person who shopped here. It wasn't right, Shelley told herself. She had to stop him.

Drawing breath deep into her lungs, she raised

her head with shaky determination and began to march toward where the man still stood eyeing the watch display, as though ready to pocket another if one caught his fancy.

She'd seen him earlier in other parts of the store. In fact, she'd begun to wonder if he was following her. He seemed to turn up everywhere she went.

Now here he was in the jewelry department, stealing watches.

He certainly didn't look like a thief. Tall and slender, he had an air of sophisticated ease that gave him the look of a gentleman. At the same time, though, Shelley thought she detected in him, just below the surface, a sense of suppressed strength and vitality, a barely leashed danger like that waiting in the shiny coils of a well-balanced bullwhip.

But then, what did a thief look like? Shelley had spent years studying to become a clinical psychologist, and she knew, if anyone did, how misleading superficial images could be. She also knew how easily perfectly normal people slipped over the edge into bizarre behavior when things went wrong in their lives.

Maybe that was the answer. With his handsome face and sense of presence he looked as though he could be an actor. Maybe he'd lost the big role, the one he'd put all his hopes on, and now, in desperation, he was retaliating against the world.

But that theory didn't hold water even as long as it took to think it up. He looked too happy for a man in despair, she thought. It had to be something else.

Maybe he was an entrepeneur who owned a chain of stores that competed with this one and he came over periodically to drive them crazy. That seemed closer to the mark. The man was having the time of his life.

He appeared to be about thirty-eight, though his looks could be misleading. His dark hair was untouched as yet by any gray, but there was an inner core of maturity and confidence to him that probably made him appear older than he was. She adjusted her estimate to thirty-five as she came up beside him.

"I think you'd better put that watch back." Her voice sounded cool and controlled. Good. Maybe he wouldn't sense how upset she was. "If you don't, I'm going to have to notify the floor manager."

His eyes were an electrifying blue that seemed to cut the air between them like lasers. She didn't know exactly what she'd expected. Anger? Resentment? Fear? In her practice she'd dealt with all those very human emotions, and many more besides. But his reaction surprised her.

He chuckled. There could be no mistake. She heard the low, rumbling sound of it distinctly. As she stood staring up into his face, her mouth agape with outrage, his hand shot out and the long fingers circled her wrist.

"Just a minute more," he told her in a low voice. "Just give it one more minute." He winked again, and the slight traces of a smile edged his full, well-defined lips, but his eyes were busy glancing about the store as though he were looking for someone, searching for something.

She stood frozen, not sure whether to challenge his hold on her or wait to see just exactly what he was up to. His fingers were warm and strong. As he turned his head she caught a slight scent of aftershave mixed with a less identifiable masculine fragrance. He was so awfully handsome, Shelley thought, his blue eyes gleaming between thick black lashes, his straight, dark hair combed tidily, his collar crisp and white. His silk tie was complemented with a gold tiepin. The trench coat looked as smooth as if someone had ironed it just that morning.

Probably a valet, she thought suddenly. Somehow he didn't have the look of a man who would iron it himself.

And yet he did have the look of a decent person. She wanted to believe the best of him. But how could she?

He held her still, but she wasn't afraid. There was nothing menacing about him. His tanned fingers gripped her wrist as a lover might, not as a captor would, and she found herself staring at the contrast between his dark skin and her own creamier tone. He was waiting for something, and she waited with him, curiosity overcoming outrage.

Curiosity had always been a weakness of hers. "You're as bad as a cat," her roommate Carrie had said more than once. "You can't keep your nose out of trouble. I only hope you've got the nine lives to go with it. With your snoopy habits you're going to need them."

Carrie wasn't the only person who'd compared her to a cat. Though her eyes were brown, they had a golden shimmer to them, and their tilted, almond shape gave her the look of a quizzical feline. Her sleek golden hair added to the image, as did her smooth, lazy way of moving her nicely rounded body.

"I'm not snoopy," she would retort when Carrie accused her. "It's purely professional interest. A psychologist better be fascinated with what people do and why they do it, or she might as well take up mechanical engineering."

So she watched as the man who held her gazed about the room, and she wondered what he was looking for.

Then his eyes met hers again and something happened. She wasn't sure just what it was, but some sort of connection was made. It was as though he knew her and she knew him on some basic, nonverbal level. The moment quivered between them, and then his attention was on the other side of the floor.

"Okay—now!" he murmured, letting go. "Call out 'thief' just as loud as you can. Make a scene."

She watched, slightly stunned, as he turned and began to stride quickly toward the escalator. "Thief," she whispered, then glanced around at the shoppers walking past.

"Thief!" she called more loudly. "Stop that man! He's taking a watch!"

People hesitated on all sides, looking about curiously, but no one made a move to stop the fleeing criminal. Shelley stared at them all, astounded. "Isn't someone going to stop him?" she cried.

The women merely gaped at her, and the nearest men began to avoid her accusing gaze.

Shelley raised her firm chin. "Then I'll do it myself," she declared, and began to run through the store in the direction the man had taken, golden hair flying out behind her. "Stop that man!" she shouted again as she caught sight of him just ahead. "Stop that thief!"

Faces blurred on either side as she dodged past the mannequins in fashion finery, but no one stepped out to help her. By now, she was motivated almost as much by her anger at the unhelpful bystanders as by the crime itself. This was what the world had come to, was it? No one ready to stand up for justice and fairness? All right. So be it. Shelley herself would become a one-woman vigilante committee.

She bounded down the moving escalator two steps at a time, pushing past the standing riders.

"You stop right there!" she cried as she came upon the tall stranger, just about to reach the heavy glass doors that led out onto the street. He turned back at the sound of her voice and she threw herself at him, "like," she would tell Carrie later when the sting of the whole affair had dimmed enough to joke about it, "an angry Scottish terrier at a disinterested Great Dane."

Taking up handfuls of trench coat to keep hold of him, she managed to foil his escape. But now that she had him, what on earth was she going to do with him?

"Someone call the manager," she called to the crowd that was gathering. "Quickly."

Yes, quickly. She looked up into his eyes and found them disconcertingly amused. "What took you so long?" he murmured for only her to hear. "I thought I was going to have to come back and do all this over again."

She straightened, releasing one hand but holding on to him with the other. Blinking up into his sparkling blue gaze, she frowned. "I don't get it," she began. "Do you mean to tell me you want to—?"

"Shhh." He put a finger to her lips. "Not now."

There wasn't time for explanations. Suddenly the store manager was there, along with two huge, uniformed policemen. Then Shelley's prisoner was emptying his pockets of the three watches, two fine calf leather wallets, and a small transistor cassette player he'd picked up during his trip through the store.

Shelley stood back, watching in confusion. Her part was over, but for some reason she couldn't turn away. She'd caught a thief, but only because he'd wanted to be caught. Now that she had time to think, she knew he could easily have pulled out of her grasp. He could have outrun her even more easily if he'd really been trying. Why would anyone want to be caught shoplifting?

"It's Miss Pride, isn't it?" One of the policemen smiled at her. She knew he'd probably seen her on one of her trips to the local station house. Her office partner did a lot of work with the department of probation, and she occasionally went along when he was called in to do psychological evaluations of prisoners.

"Yes," she answered, surprised to hear the tremor in her voice. She gripped her hands tightly together to stop the shaking. "Yes, it is."

"And you're the one who nabbed this guy, huh?" He grinned at her. "You won't mind coming downtown to give us a statement, will you?"

She looked at the prisoner, wincing as she saw the handcuffs being placed around his wrists. His face was casually unconcerned and she had a quick feeling that the sight of the shiny metal against his warm flesh hurt her more than it did him. "No," she answered hoarsely. "No, I won't mind at all."

The next thing she knew, she was riding in the passenger seat of the squad car with one officer while the mysterious thief sat in the back with the other. Shelley sat stiffly, uncomfortably aware of the man just behind her. Why had he done it? And why had he entangled her in his plot, whatever it was?

There was something compelling about him, about his elegant good looks, his casual sophistication, his incongruous crime. She'd love to get him on the couch.

She had to bite her lip to hold back a quick surge of laughter, knowing she'd made a definite Freudian slip. Hastily she corrected her observation: She would love to get a crack at analyzing his motivations. That's what she'd meant. But she had to admit she hadn't exactly been blind to his masculine charms.

That didn't really worry her though. She was used to suppressing feelings of that sort. Shelley Pride had a very well-ordered life. Her work was very important to her. Men had no place in her current scheme of things. As casual escorts now and then, maybe. But nothing serious.

"This will only take a few minutes," the policeman assured her. "Then I'll drive you back out to get your car."

She nodded and glanced back. A pair of bright blue eyes met hers, and the man smiled as though he knew every secret thought in her mind.

She flushed and looked away quickly. There was something about him that had disturbed her from the beginning. She remembered the first contact she'd had with him that morning. It had been in the stationery department while she was looking for a birthday card for Jerry Kramer, the psychologist she shared a suite of offices with. She'd searched the rack, frowning with impatience, coming up with one clichéd greeting card after another, and suddenly a hand appeared before her face, handing her a card she hadn't seen.

Birthdays are precious, it said. *Each one deserves to be saved in a special place.* The picture showed a little boy hiding his pet frog under his bed—along with his slingshot and snail collection. It was perfect for Jerry.

She whirled, looking for the man who'd given her the card, but he was disappearing around a corner, and all she saw was the expensive cut of his trench coat and the soft shine of his nearly black hair.

She was sure, however, that it was the same man who came sauntering through Designer Fashions a bit later and caught her trying on an elegant, off-the-shoulder gown that she had no intention of buying. It cost at least a month's salary and was a direct contrast to the business clothes she usually wore. Even today, taking a morning off from office work, she was dressed in a plain plaid skirt and kelly green short-sleeved cotton sweater. No one would ever mistake her for a femme fatale.

That was what one would need to be to wear a dress like the delicious creation she'd seen on the rack. She had picked it up on a whim, turning the garment slowly, wondering who could afford such an extravagance. But she'd felt only a twinge of guilt as with assumed casualness she asked the saleswoman if she might try it on.

The saleswoman had given her a penetrating look, then a tight smile, and Shelley decided she'd passed some sort of secret test. Maybe she looked like she could afford jet-set clothes. The very thought made her giggle. At any rate the saleswoman graciously set out the gown for her, helped her zip the back, and escorted her to the thickly carpeted, multimirrored nook where she could see herself from all angles.

Her honey-gold hair was cut in a layered curtain that hung to her shoulders, the sides brushed back like feathered wings. The style was too young and casual for the gown. She should have her hair swept up in a chignon with tiny curls around her face and long diamond earrings swaying at either side. That would go much better with the boysenberry silk pleated dress that felt so luxurious against her naked skin.

What would it be like to actually wear clothes like this? she wondered. To go to balls and parties on yachts and sip champagne with the fast, moneyed crowd? Shelley smiled at her reflection, noting her own wide, honest brown eyes and slightly freckled nose, which still made her look like a bit of a tomboy for all her twenty-six years of age. Hardly the face one might find at the fashionable watering holes, she admitted to herself, a twinkle glinting in her glance. Not that things like that had ever mattered to her.

The saleswoman stepped off to help another customer, and Shelley was left alone with the gown and her reflection in the flattering mirrors. Tilting her head back, she narrowed her eyes until the picture before her faded into a gauzy fantasy, and she let her body sway slightly to the rhythm of a make-believe waltz.

She could almost hear the band playing. "One two three—dum-de-de . . ." she whispered to herself. Throwing caution to the winds, she began the slow box step, side to side and back, side to side and back, and then, ludicrously, right into the arms of the mysterious stranger.

As she went limp with shock he continued the pattern, holding her up from behind like a giant rag doll. "La-la-la-lalala," he hummed into her hair, the tune right out of a Vienna dance hall. "La-la-la-lalala . . ."

The humming was his, but she realized, to her chagrin, that the gurgling sound of total confusion was all her own. Struggling to regain her balance, she pushed away from him. "I—I'm sorry," she stammered, pulling her dress straight, not really sure if she should apologize to him for reckless waltzing or cry foul for his interference.

But she didn't have time to do either. He stepped away with only a quick, knowing smile and a murmured, "It's lovely on you. I say take it, by all means," before disappearing around another convenient corner.

And then she'd found him heisting watches in the jewelry department. Just who was this masked man anyway?

The station house was long and modern with charcoal-gray walls and tall windows of tinted glass. The officer who'd driven escorted Shelley in through the crowded lobby. Telephones screamed, voices ricocheted in confusion from wall to austere wall, people moved in a kaleidoscope of style and color; but Shelley wasn't overwhelmed. She'd been here before.

"Have a seat right here," the patrolman offered, pointing out a collection of bedraggled couches grouped around a small coffee table covered with torn magazines. "I'll have a clerk come and take your statement."

She turned to watch where they were taking the shoplifter and saw him disappear down a corridor, flanked by the other officer who'd been in on the arrest and two men in business suits. Collared by the long arm of the law, she thought irrelevantly. A shiver tickled her spine as she wondered if they were going to put him in a holding cell. Just the sound of the words was so dehumanizing.

But she really had nothing else to do with that end of the case. As far as she was concerned, it was all over. She would make her report and get back to work.

Glancing at the silver watch on her slender wrist, she grimaced. Jerry would certainly be wondering what was keeping her. She'd taken the morning off in an unusual fit of restlessness. But it was Tuesday, the day she set aside for studying professional journals and working on papers. She had no appointments to rush back for. She had all the time in the world. So she sat and waited.

And waited and waited. And the longer she waited, the more she began to worry about her thief.

That was the way she thought of him now. Her thief. After all, she was the one who'd made sure he was arrested. Never mind that he seemed to have wanted it that way.

What were they doing to him now? She knew that modern police ethics weren't supposed to include any strong-arm tactics, and she'd spent enough time at the station house herself to know that they treated their job just as professionally as anyone else, but for some reason old scenes from Jimmy Cagney movies kept floating into her mind.

Giving them the third degree, they used to call it. Surely they wouldn't resort to that, she scoffed, laughing at herself. But pictures of snarling faces, blinding lights, blackened eyes, and swollen jaws kept surfacing.

And then there were the unanswered questions. Why had a man like that been shoplifting? And why had he purposefully drawn her into his scheme? She would dearly love to delve for more clues to the answers. Purely professional curiosity, she told herself sternly. Nothing more.

She got up and paced, ignoring the pandemonium as people streamed by. After two cups of stale coffee from the office machine and three trips to the front desk to see what was holding things up, a clerk finally appeared and asked Shelley to follow her to a "consulting room."

Shelley trailed the short woman out again through the noisy lobby, then down the corridor the others had taken.

"Go down to the third door on your left," said the clerk, whose blond curls and dimpled cheeks made her look like a valentine cherub. "Let me grab a form and I'll be right back to take your statement."

Shelley took a step toward her destination, but the sound of laughter turned her attention to the open doorway she was passing. As she looked in, her gaze met the laughing eyes of her thief.

He was sitting back in a padded swivel chair situated at the head of a long table, totally at ease, holding a tall, icy drink in his hand, while a group of men, some in uniform, some not, sat around the table, looking for all the world like an appreciative audience. He'd obviously just told a very funny joke, for all the men were laughing, while he sat smiling before them, looking very pleased with himself.

As she hesitated at the door, staring into his eyes, he winked again.

Jimmy Cagney, indeed! Life seemed to be one long comedy to this man. To think she'd wasted her worry on him. While she, the innocent witness, was left cooling her heels, the "criminal" was being feted in a back room like a hero! She wanted to throw something at his head. Just exactly what was going on here?

"Miss Pride!"

The blond clerk was already back and waiting. Shelley swallowed her outrage and marched down the corridor, suppressing her instinct to rant at the woman. It was hardly her fault. But that didn't make Shelley feel any friendlier toward the mysterious stranger.

She gave her statement easily enough. With a definite feeling of vengeful satisfaction, she went back over all the details of the crime. She hoped they'd lock him away for years—well, hours at least, just on the strength of her testimony. The clerk typed furiously, then handed her a copy to read and sign and requested that she wait in the lobby once again.

She walked down the hallway, but this time the door was closed, and she couldn't hear any clues as to what was going on inside. She paused for just a moment at the doorway, then resolutely turned away and strode to the battered couches. Impatiently she sat down on the edge of the cushion. It was time to get on with her day. She'd wasted too much energy on this crazy situation already.

"Hi." Suddenly her thief was standing before her, his trench coat draped over his arm, his blue eyes twinkling. "Let's go, shall we?" He gestured toward the lobby with a toss of his head.

Shelley rose uncertainly from the couch. Let's go, he'd said, but surely he meant on to another conference room, or to the sergeant's desk, or to a judge's chambers. Perhaps he'd been sent to get her. . . .

She didn't have time to think things through before he took her by the elbow and began propelling her through the crowd. "Sorry about the delay," he murmured, his breath teasing her hair, "but you know how these agencies are. Nothing but red tape."

There it was again—the indefinable sense of connection. As though she were in on the joke with him. As though the pictures in her mind fit with those in his in some bewildering jigsaw to form something whole for him. Why couldn't she see them the way he could?

Her mind was so filled with questions, and her senses were so filled with the overall awareness of him, that he had her out the front door of the station and halfway down the wide front steps before she realized where they were going.

"Wait a minute," she insisted, hanging back, and at the same time a voice came from behind them.

"Aren't you forgetting something, Harper?"

Her thief turned toward the speaker slowly, his hand still controlling Shelley's elbow. They both looked up at the man standing at the top of the stairs. "Caught again," her thief said ruefully. "That's twice in one day. My mother told me there'd be days like this."

Shelley glared at him, trying to pull away from his grasp, but not having a lot of luck at the attempt. "I'll bet you have a lot of them," she snapped, wishing she didn't feel so totally at sea. What was going on here? She'd almost run off with a criminal!

The two of them remounted the steps while Shelley looked searchingly at the man waiting for them at the glass door. He was tall and thin, with a dark, gaunt look. She was sure she'd seen him at the station before, but she wasn't sure who he was.

"Is it always so easy for your prisoners to escape?" she asked, a bit flustered by all the confusion and taking it out on the stranger at the door.

"I'm surprised the city hasn't been taken over by thugs."

The man managed a stiff smile. "There are those who claim that's exactly what did happen in the last election," he responded dryly. "But I have to demur, Miss Pride. After all, a less trusting soul than I might be ready to accuse you of aiding and abetting in this case."

Shelley flushed, but before she could come to her own defense, her thief answered for her.

"Not a chance, Sam. This is the good citizen who turned me in. She had no idea I was trying to lead her astray."

The man he'd designated as Sam held the door for the two of them to reenter the building. "She couldn't see where she was going?" he asked skeptically as he followed them in.

"Blinded by my charm, Sam," the thief answered jovially. "Blinded by my charm."

Shelley looked from one to the other of her escorts with perplexity, not sure what to make of what had just happened, nor what to think of their good-natured bantering. "Just exactly who are you?" she asked the tall dark man at last, as he took her free arm. She had an odd sensation of being the rope in a tug-of-war. "And where are you taking me?"

"Do you mean to tell me you two haven't met?" Her thief looked shocked at such a breach of etiquette. "Shelley Pride, meet Detective Sam Gladstone. He's the right man to cultivate in this precinct. Knows all the best restaurants."

They stopped before the sergeant's desk, but Shelley turned to look at the man who puzzled her so. "You know who I am?" she asked.

He nodded. "I was filled in. They know all about you here." He winked. "Could be that somewhere in the files there's a hidden dossier containing every secret of your young life."

Sam's growl stopped that discourse, but Shelley still wasn't satisfied. "Just who are you?" she asked her thief forthrightly. "And why do you seem to run around here like you own the place?"

He glanced from her to the dour detective. "Michael Harper's the name," he told her smoothly. "And right now, shoplifting's my game."

Looking at him, she suddenly knew she didn't believe a word of it. "I hope you're not planning to make a living at it," she said tartly. "You're really not very good."

He grinned. "But that's just the point," he said softly. "I'm not supposed to be."

The detective cleared his throat and Michael raised an eyebrow. "I think Sam has some papers he wants us to sign," he said. "Then we can get out of here." He sighed. "Though I must say, I think you're being a bit overzealous about this, Sam."

Shelley frowned, still sunk in confusion, but Sam moved forward and took the sheaf of papers from the sergeant's hands. "It doesn't pay to be careless. This is for your own protection." He assumed a more formal tone. "We're releasing Michael Harper on his own recognizance, provided he agrees to a complete psychological evaluation. It has been determined that his crimes are very likely the result of stress and overwork rather than pro-clivity for thievery. The department store has agreed to drop charges if he agrees to seek help." He held out a pen. "Sign here, Harper. And will you please sign for your partner, Miss Pride?"

Shelley looked down at the form she was expected to apply her signature to. It certified that Jerry Kramer would provide psychological coun-seling for Michael Harper and would report any noncompliance on the part of the patient. A com-plete report was to be submitted within six weeks and a review of the case would be made by the department at that time. The man was going to come to her office for testing. She remembered, suddenly, how she'd wanted to get him on the couch herself. Luckily this would be Jerry's problem.

Nagging curiosity still lurked somewhere inside, but she was fighting it. Maybe there were some things best left unanalyzed.

She signed quickly, ready to duck out of the building, but as she turned to ask Sam Gladstone if she could leave, and if someone would be available to take her back to the department-store parking lot where she'd left her car, she felt the strong hand on her elbow again.

"I'll see that Miss Pride gets back to her car," Michael Harper told the detective. He glanced smoothly at the expensive-looking watch on his wrist. "And I think I'll take care that she's fed a good lunch as well. She deserves it after all she's been through today."

Shelley tried to draw away, amazed at how confidently the man thought he could take over. "I don't need any help, or any lunch," she protested. "I can take care of myself."

He refused to let go of her elbow. Looking at her, he sighed deeply. "Tell her I'm harmless, Sam," he pleaded. "Make her love me."

Sam made a noise that sounded suspiciously like a snort. "I wouldn't advise you hand your life over to him, Miss," he said grudgingly. "But I think you can trust him with your afternoon."

Shelley wasn't about to trust him with anything. She had things to do, places to go, people to see, and they had nothing to do with handsome shoplifters who seemed to be in cahoots with the local police in some strange way. Even for curiosity's sake she wasn't going to get involved.

Raising her eyes to Michael's, she was prepared to tell him just that, and in no uncertain terms. But it happened again. The connection was made, and it sizzled. This time it felt almost as though something was flowing between them. And instead of stomping off in a huff, she found herself walking docilely beside him, out the door, and down the steps. Was he taking over her mind?

Two

Even though Shelley seemed to have lost her will to resist his guidance, she hadn't quite lost her ability to voice objections.

"Where are we going?" she asked suspiciously as Michael propelled her through the parking lot and out onto the sidewalk. "Where are you taking me?"

"To lunch, of course," he answered, smiling down at her. "It's way past your mealtime. I can tell. You're getting peckish."

"Peckish!" She had a rough idea what the word meant, and she knew she didn't like it applied to herself. "I'm not a bit peckish."

"You most certainly are," he insisted with maddening good nature. "I know the signs well." He cocked an eyebrow. "Short temper. Flashing eyes. Diminishing sense of humor. You're a classic case."

Despite her misgivings, she felt her mouth relaxing into an answering smile. "And you're a major diagnostician, I suppose," she replied, but there was no sting in her words.

They stopped to wait for a light to turn green. He reached up his free hand to straighten the knot in his silk tie with easy pride. "One of my many talents," he admitted. "I've often been told I'm a master at analyzing these things, and even more adept at prescribing the perfect cure."

The light changed and they walked on, steps matching perfectly despite his much longer legs.

Shelley caught a glimpse of their reflection as they passed a bright storefront. Michael looked cool and sophisticated. His bearing had a casual elegance that was uniquely complemented by his perfect suit, while she . . . what could she say? She looked like a college girl in her plaid skirt and nubby sweater. Even her freckles seemed to stand out, branding her for what she was. Funny how she'd never noticed it before. She looked young and careless and out of place at Michael's side. Pretty, she thought with sudden anxiety, but naive.

"What's the cure for peckishness?" she asked, as much to banish the thoughts of inadequacy from her mind as to find the answer.

"Sushi," he answered with sublime aplomb.

"Sushi?" She stopped dead in the center of the sidewalk, heedless of the people pushing past. "You mean, that Japanese stuff?"

He nodded. "Exactly."

She shook her head slowly, her dark eyes wide. "No, I'm not really hungry. Actually, now that I think about it, I really should get back to work. If you'll just . . ." Her words trailed off as she looked wildly up and down the street, hoping forlornly for a taxi. If she'd realized he was going to try to make her eat weird food, she'd never have thought twice about refusing lunch, sizzling connection or not.

The ghost of an impatient frown feathered between his brows. "Don't you like sushi?"

She swallowed. She'd heard about sushi, and as she remembered it, the news had not been good. The words *raw fish* and *seaweed* seemed to stick in her memory. "I don't know," she admitted. "I've never tried it."

Michael looked thunderstruck. "Never tried sushi? Here you live in California, the land of the instant fad, and you've let one of the biggest ones slip away?"

Shelley tried for a haughty look and knew she'd failed by the gleam in his blue eyes. "I don't pay any attention to fads," she told him. "I'm much too busy for that kind of thing."

He dismissed what she'd said with a wave of his hand and took her by the elbow again, walking with a long, sure stride that had her jogging beside him like an eager puppy. "No one is too busy for this kind of thing," he informed her sunnily. "Sam recommended a sushi bar in the next block. You're in for an educational experience."

She tried to defend her reputation for tolerance. "I love sukiyaki. And tempura."

He wasn't buying it. "That's for dinner. Sushi makes a better lunch."

"But I'm not hungry," she tried rather lamely.

"That's irrelevant," he retorted. "A sushi bar is a feast for all senses, not just taste. You can sit back and watch the interplay of subtle colors, smell the exotic food, listen to the delicate samisen music—"

"And watch you stuff yourself, I suppose." She sniffed, knowing she was losing the fight. "Sounds delightful."

But there was no more time for protest. Michael was leading her in through a doorway marked by a bright cotton banner, and before she had a chance to think of a new means of escape, she was seated at the long, blue-tiled counter, staring into the eyes of a man who looked for all the world like a Samurai warrior, sword and all.

"We'll need just a moment to discuss our order," Michael told him, testing the air with anticipation. "What'll it be, Shelley? Squid? Octopus? Abalone?"

"I told you I wasn't hungry." Shelley was gripping the edge of the counter as though afraid she wouldn't be able to stay in her seat without help. She wasn't sure why the thought of this strange food terrified her so, but she knew she'd never make it through a meal of it.

Suddenly she found Michael's hand covering hers. "Hey," he said softly, a puzzled look in his eyes, "don't worry. I'm not going to force-feed you." His fingers tightened. "We'll go somewhere else."

She felt color flooding her cheeks. Great, she thought. Just the thing for a freckled face. A nice rosy background to make the freckles stand out like ants on a picnic cloth. She'd been acting awfully silly and she knew it. Somehow she had to erase the image of skittish filly she knew was being implanted in Michael's mind. Forcing back her feelings of fear, she managed a tremulous smile.

"Don't be ridiculous," she said as breezily as she could. "This is fine. I'll just have some tea and watch you"—she couldn't hold back a quick shudder—"eat."

He hesitated, then grinned. "Good girl. But we won't make you watch the sushi preparation. Not this time." He called over the sushi chef, ordered something incomprehensible, and asked him to deliver the order to a table on the other side of the room.

"A secluded booth," he said softly to her as he led her to it. "You won't have to watch how sushi is made, and others won't be able to watch what we're up to."

Though she'd felt a strong attraction between the two of them all along, this was the first time he'd hinted at feeling the slightest romantic interest. She threw him a startled look and purposefully slid only halfway across the red plastic seat, leaving no room for him on her side of the table. He sighed, but didn't make an issue of it as he sat down across from her.

A waitress quickly followed, serving them tea and bowing gracefully as she backed away.

"Now," Michael said firmly, leaning forward to look deeply into her eyes, "tell me all about yourself. How does a psychologist come to be so afraid of trying anything new?"

She stared back at him, thrown off-guard by his direct approach. It wasn't really true. On the whole she was as ready as anyone for new experiences. Wasn't she? Suddenly she realized just how long she'd been caught up in her work, totally immersed in it. Maybe it was time she took a little pause for reassessment. But this was hardly the time to think about that.

So instead of answering, she came through with a counterpunch. "First you explain to me how a shoplifter comes to be so buddy-buddy with the police," she asked tartly.

His laugh was soft and low. "Criminals and cops have a symbiotic relationship. Just like those little birds that live on top of hippos in the wild. We couldn't do without each other."

There was more to it than that. She'd sensed it before, and she could see it in his eyes now. She very much wanted to get to the bottom of this mystery.

"You're not really a shoplifter, are you?" she guessed. "What were you doing in that department store today?"

His smile faded a bit. "I hope the man I created that charade for isn't as perceptive as you are," he answered. "If he is, all will have been in vain."

"Ah-hah," she pounced. "So it was for show. But why?"

He stretched back in his seat, a smile on his face. "Send a thief to catch a thief, they always say. There was a man—his identity is unimportant—working on that floor, who badly needed proof that I have sticky fingers. And so I was providing it for him." He chuckled. "You wouldn't believe how many things I picked up right under people's noses, and no one said a thing. Until I found you."

A light went off in her memory. "He was the one you were looking for when you made me wait before accusing you out loud."

He grinned. "And you waited too. That surprised me. One look at your determined face and I thought the show was going to be all over before the audience arrived."

The waitress appeared at their table with the food, giving Shelley a reprieve from having to explain how he'd fascinated her, how she'd been consumed with curiosity about him and his strange activities. She sat back in the seat, watching with wary apprehension as the waitress set a beautiful black lacquer tray in front of Michael. Strange things were sitting in little mounds on the tray, and she avoided looking directly at them. She felt almost as though she were sitting across from someone who was gleefully looking forward to consuming live ants on a stick, followed by a chaser of wriggling earthworms.

"For you," the delicate waitress said, bowing as she set a small porcelain dish before Shelley. In the center, artfully surrounded by slivers of white vegetable and coils of orange ginger, lay a long, black cylinder, cut across into slices like a very small jelly roll. "California roll," she announced with pride. "You will like it, please."

Shelley recoiled, ready to insist that she wasn't

hungry and was not about to touch anything in this restaurant, but when her eyes met the hopeful gaze of the waitress, she swallowed her words. "I'm sure I will," she replied weakly. "Thank you."

Michael was grinning at her as the waitress departed. "Don't worry," he said. "Not a piece of raw fish has even breathed near that roll. If you'll look carefully, you'll see that the vinegared rice is wrapped around nothing more threatening than nice pink, well-cooked shrimp and green avocado."

She looked down and saw what he was talking about. "That may be," she said suspiciously, "but what is this paper-thin black stuff on the outside?"

A vague shadow passed over his face. "Just taste it and . . ."

Shelley gave him a look of long-suffering patience. "What is it?" she demanded gently.

He sighed. "Seaweed. But it's delicious, believe me. Just try it."

She poked at a slice of it with a single chopstick, feeling very silly for her irrational fear. A psychologist should be above these things, she told herself. A psychologist should have her life under control. She'd thought she did. But maybe that was because she'd been swimming along in her own stream, unchallenged by any unusual currents. Looking into Michael's eyes, she thought she could see hints of a whole ocean of wild water waiting just beyond.

"Come on," he urged softly. "Be brave."

She flashed him a searing glance. "Bravery has nothing to do with it," she lied. "I'm just not very hungry." But she knew she couldn't get away with that much longer. Clutching both chopsticks in her hand, she gingerly picked up a thick slice and, holding her breath, nibbled at a few kernels of rice.

"You were telling me about your crime," she reminded him, hoping to take his mind off how she was coping with the unusual food. Actually the rice wasn't half bad. She took another nibble, this time snagging a piece of plump shrimp and a dash of avocado. "Do you work for the police?"

He shrugged. "Not exactly. I'm with the district attorney's office. And since I've just moved into this territory after five years in the Bay Area, the local police, except for Sam, didn't know who I was at first."

She realized she'd devoured the whole slice of California roll without a qualm. Her stomach hadn't made one protest. Even the delicate sea-weed covering tasted good. Not sealike at all. She picked up a second slice and began work on it.

Michael handled the wooden eating utensils with the same deft grace that seemed to come naturally to everything he did, Shelley noticed. She found herself watching him, studying little things, like the way the corners of his mouth seemed to tug into a smile almost against his will, and the way he narrowed his eyes when enjoying a special taste—or looking at her.

It was true, she realized with a start. He was enjoying looking at her. She could see the telltale signs. Suddenly she found her own mouth curving into an unbidden smile as well. It had been so long since she'd noticed a man in this way—noticed him noticing her—she'd forgotten how nice it could feel.

"What are you, then?" she challenged him. "An undercover agent, or what?"

He glanced around the room with lazy chagrin. "Not so loud, if you please," he reminded as he put a cloth napkin to his lips and reached for his round teacup. "This is not a piece of information meant for public knowledge. In fact, Sam wouldn't be pleased at all that I've told you."

Her gaze met his sparkling blue eyes, and she knew it was a game to him; a big, funny, exciting game. And he was confident of winning every time. She couldn't help but laugh back at him.

"But you know you can trust me," she told him. "Right?"

He chuckled aloud. "No, now that you mention it, I don't know anything of the kind. But I thought you deserved to know the truth, after the award-winning performance you played for me today."

The smile faded from her face. She remembered how frightened she'd been, how she'd had to steel herself to do what she thought was her duty. "That wasn't a performance," she told him softly. "I thought you were for real. I wanted you stopped."

"And you did the job beautifully. Sarah Bernhardt, eat your heart out."

She gazed at him levelly, realizing how different their memories were of the event they'd shared. She remembered the fear, the anxiety. She was glad no one had been hurt, and she wondered how often innocent bystanders did fall victim to the sort of game Michael played.

Meanwhile Michael remembered the thrill, the triumph of a plan well executed. Were other people merely pawns to him?

She shook her head. What did it matter? He wasn't going to be her patient, but Jerry's.

"I didn't know the district attorney did this kind of thing," she commented. "I thought that was left to the FBI."

He smiled. "We work in connection with them, just as we do with the local police. You see, there's a new emphasis on white-collar crime, especially in areas like the Gold Coast, the Newport-Balboa area of Orange County, which are full of new money and people who like to speculate with it. We're working under a special federal law-enforcement grant. We're kind of a penthouse bunco squad."

"White-collar crime?"

"Swindles. Real estate scams. Investment fraud.

Setting up suckers where they have to throw in a lot of money to reach a tempting goal, but somewhere down the line the goal evaporates on them, and they never get their money back. In the past that sort of thing has been prosecuted on a hit-or-miss basis, changing attorneys with the changing seasons. What we're trying to do is set up a separate unit of investigators and attorneys who will stay with each case from undercover work right on through conviction and sentencing."

His eyes were shining as he talked, and she could see he loved his job. "So you were working on the undercover stage when we ran into each other. But why did the police go through with the charade of sticking you in counseling for six months?" she asked curiously.

He shrugged, chasing a stray chip of ginger around the edge of his lacquer tray with his chopsticks. "It's all part of the attempt at verisimilitude. I'll show up for the first few appointments, but once this case is closed, I'll drop out."

She cocked her head to the side, looking at him speculatively. "Maybe you ought to take this opportunity to get some real help," she told him, not noticing how his brows drew together at her suggestion. "Jerry . . . I mean, Doctor Kramer's very good at psychotherapy."

"What makes you think I might need psychotherapy?" The low silkiness of the voice warned her he hadn't taken kindly to her idea. He'd abandoned his lunch and was staring at her with very little humor left in his eyes.

"Everyone can use a sounding board now and then," she covered vaguely. "You know, this California roll is really very good." She popped the last bite into her mouth and chewed on it innocently, glancing almost surreptitiously to see what Michael had left on his plate. The roll hadn't been large at all, and she was still hungry.

"Why don't you give me some analysis?" His hand reached across the table, suddenly covering hers. She tried to draw away, a bit startled and a lot disturbed by the familiarity, the warmth. But he held tightly, and the tease was back in his eyes. "I'll have the appointments set up with you instead of Doctor Kramer. I'm sure you could help me uncover all my neuroses in record time."

"I can't do it," she squeaked out, embarrassed by the shakiness of her voice. "I'm not a fully qualified psychologist yet. I'm only interning."

He raised an eyebrow. "Just a baby shrink, are you?"

She stumbled on quickly, trying to explain. "I do some counseling. I've got a limited license as a therapist. And I teach a night class at the local junior college on Thursday nights. But I can't take contract work from government agencies." She drew her tongue across her lips. "You see, I've completed all my classwork, but I've got a certain amount of intern hours to fulfill, and my thesis to complete, before I'm a full-fledged clinical psychologist."

"I see." His fingers moved on hers with easy, seductive power. She felt as though he were about to reel her in, arm first. "And just what does your thesis deal with?"

She couldn't seem to take her eyes off his hard, brown fingers, but she kept talking as quickly as she could. "The psychology of color as related to dietary habits," she explained, putting her mouth on automatic. "You see, the color of food has so much to do with how we perceive it, how we taste. So I've conducted countless experiments. I cook macaroni in red food coloring, green scrambled eggs, purple applesauce, and I set up test feedings, studying how appetites change when confronted with unconventionally colored food."

"Green eggs?" he asked, his face contorted in horror.

She nodded. "Black mashed potatoes, orange milk."

He let her hand go in a rush of laughter. "Incredible," he sputtered. "And you have the nerve to turn up your nose at sushi?"

"Oh, but that's totally different," she protested, and then sank back in her seat, realizing it wasn't at all.

He slid across the seat and rose from the table. "Shelley Pride," he announced, reaching down and putting a finger under her chin to tilt her face up toward his. "I find you quite delightful, but I'm going to have to ask you to excuse me for a moment. I have a telephone call to make, and it can't wait."

Still smiling, he leaned down and dropped a light kiss on her lips, and then turned and left her to stare after him in pleased astonishment.

She liked him. A slow smile spread across her face as she whispered the words aloud. She liked Michael Harper. Liked him very much. Why didn't that scare her?

It should. She hadn't felt so strongly attracted to a man since—Lord, she could hardly remember when. Barry, probably, and their romance had flowered during her senior year of college, while she was trying to decide whether to go on to graduate school and starve, or get a job and make a decent living for a change.

She'd ended up doing both, working as a secretary in the day and going to night school to finish her degree. And that was why it had taken her so long to get to the verge of earning her full professional credentials. At the time her disillusionment with Barry had helped to make her decision easier.

He'd been a loving friend, with thick, curly red hair and serious green eyes that seemed to say he loved her. His lips said the same thing, not to mention his body. And she'd been so sure they would marry when they graduated.

It wasn't until she'd thought she'd surprise him by finding an apartment for the two of them to share after the wedding that she'd met his other girlfriend. Lydia, his very pregnant live-in lover, about whom Shelley had never heard a whisper.

Once the truth was out, she could look back and see all the signs she'd blithely ignored before. The way he'd avoided taking her to his rooms at a nearby boarding house, the nights he'd been too busy "studying" to see her, the fact that he claimed he didn't have a telephone. His life with her had been restricted to on-campus. He'd lived another life in town.

"I need you both," he'd protested when she'd confronted him. "I need the intellectual stimulation I get from you, the earthy mothering I get from Lydia. Why can't women accept these things?"

Why, indeed? A strange thing happened to Shelley. Her love for Barry evaporated, overwhelmed by her new friendship with Lydia. She and the shy girl joined forces, and Shelley was there to witness Lydia and Barry's wedding. She was also there to help when the baby first came, and to wave farewell when the little family packed up and left for Oregon, destined for a small farm near Eugene.

And now, here was Michael Harper, stirring the embers of old excitements. She shook her head, smiling at her own silliness. She mustn't take this too seriously, she told herself. Better to put her mind on something else.

Something like food. She glanced down at her empty plate, then across at the little mounds left in Michael's lacquer tray. The California roll seemed better and better the more she thought about it. How different could the sushi Michael ordered be?

She reached over with her chopsticks and poked at one mound, testing the thin piece of white, flaky material lying on top of the rice. Michael was right. If she could face black mashed potatoes without a quiver, how could she cringe at raw fish? Looking around quickly to make sure no one was watching, she broke off a tiny piece and put it on her tongue, shuddering slightly as she did so.

No taste. She moved it around in her mouth experimentally. No taste at all. Maybe she needed a bigger piece.

Getting really brave now, she took a larger bite and chewed it thoughtfully. There was a taste, but it wasn't the least bit fishy. In fact, it was so delicate, so light, the meat seemed to melt in her mouth. Full of confidence, she picked up the rest of the mound—vinegared rice, raw fish, and all—and popped it in her mouth.

Delicious. It tasted like the restaurant smelled, slightly exotic, but very good. She wanted more.

Stretching out across the table, she studied the contents of the tray. She quickly ruled out one little goody. From the rubbery look of the meat, she was sure it must be octopus. She could still see where the suckers had been. Even in her newly tolerant state, that was a little too much for her. But there were others. Maybe the pink fish with the silvery sheen . . .

"Ah-hah!" Michael's voice went through her like an electric shock, and she jumped back guiltily. "I knew I was a fool to trust you too easily. A woman who would take the food right out of a man's mouth!"

"It wasn't anywhere near your mouth," she retorted, pretending to pout. "And anyway, you were the one who wanted me to open my mind."

He dropped down into the seat and slid the entire tray over to her side of the table. "Feel free," he told her. "I'm glad to think I've done my part to promote world peace and international understanding."

She grinned a bit sheepishly, but she didn't turn down his offer. "I don't think I can do much to affect world peace," she admitted. "But if eating good food helps, I'll certainly try to do my part."

He sat back and watched her eat, his eyes warm and amused. Looking up, she met his gaze and suddenly felt as though she had a mouth too full of oatmeal. Swallowing carefully, she tried to get him talking again.

"Did you reach the party you were phoning?"

He nodded, not saying a word, just watching her. She remembered what he'd said before. "I find you quite delightful" had been his exact words. His eyes were saying the same thing in their own way.

It was very exciting, but she knew it was also an exercise in danger. Get him talking, she told herself. Quick, before you begin to believe what his eyes are saying.

Groping, she came back to the phone call. "Well, did they give you a new cloak-and-dagger assignment?" she asked, her voice slightly high. "Are you heading off to try shoplifting in other parts of the country?"

His eyes darkened seriously. "My work isn't something I can joke about in public, Shelley," he said quietly.

She sat back, a bit stung by his rebuke. Of course, it wasn't; she should have known better. "How long have you been at this . . . profession?" she asked in a softer voice, glancing around to make sure there was no one within earshot.

He shrugged his wide shoulders. "It seems like all my life."

"Is it dangerous?"

His face broke into a smile. "Your eyes are so big.

No, it's not very dangerous. Not any more so than high-rise construction work or hang gliding."

It was obviously very dangerous. And just as obvious, that was part of what he loved about it. She felt a vague wave of regret. Pity the poor woman who fell in love with Michael Harper.

"I suppose you have to move a lot."

He nodded. "It's best to keep the territory fresh. That way the targets don't know who you are."

"And relationships don't get too demanding?" she guessed with sudden insight. That was probably another thing he liked about the job. There was always a good excuse for moving on.

"Relationships don't even exist," he informed her with a jaunty smile. "I can't afford to get too close to anyone. Not only is the time too short, the barriers one tends to let down in such a situation could render one vulnerable to . . . others."

My God, Shelley thought, staring at him openmouthed. Didn't he realize what he was doing? He was a prime candidate for severe psychological problems if he kept this up. Talk about avoidance rationalization! Talk about the Peter Pan complex! Maybe a few sessions with Jerry would do him some good after all.

"I can read your mind, lady shrink," he informed her with a groan. "And you can forget it. I'm a perfectly normal, happy man. And I don't need a psychologist to tell me otherwise."

"I didn't say a word." She blinked at him innocently. "Not a word." But she would say plenty to Jerry when she got the chance.

Yes, she decided as she finished every bit of the sushi, except for the mound covered with a thin slice of octopus, and drank her tea. Yes, her earlier feeling had been right. Pity the poor woman who fell in love with Michael Harper.

It was a good thing she was immune. Oh, she liked him. In fact, she liked him very much. And his potent masculine appeal was undeniable. But she'd spent years slowly building the solid wall she lived behind, and she really had no fear that it would shatter in this one encounter. And, as he'd said himself, she probably wouldn't see him again.

Three

They left the tiny sushi bar and went to the curb to hail a cab. Shelley watched with a twinge of resentment as a yellow car sped to their side the moment Michael called it. That was the sort of man he was, Shelley thought: one who could produce anything he wanted with a snap of his fingers. She spent agonized eons trying to shout down a taxi every time she was stranded. Michael had only to lift a hand.

The ride back to the department store was short, but Michael kept her laughing all the way, giving a running travelogue of Orange County streets as they went. The taxi dropped them at her car, and she noticed Michael seemed to take it for granted that she would be giving him a ride.

"Where are you parked?" she asked as he settled onto the velour seat of her silver-blue Cougar.

"I'm not," he replied cheerfully. "I don't usually

leave loose ends flapping behind me when I work. Why don't we just go on back to your office? I can call for my car from there and make my first appointment with your partner at the same time."

Perfectly logical, Shelley thought. Why not? But somehow she felt an edge of apprehension. She'd spent an enjoyable afternoon with a man she probably would never see again, and she'd spent it as a woman, not as a professional psychologist. Once back at the office, the woman would have to retreat while the professional took over. How would Michael relate to that?

He seemed to do just fine. She was the one who developed the problem. The reception lobby opened onto the parking lot, and as they walked in Shelley found herself flushing slightly. What was this? Was she embarrassed to bring him here? Or was she embarrassed to have her colleagues see how much she liked him? She wasn't sure what it was and, luckily for her, there was no one in the lobby to test it.

"Maria, our secretary, must be in with Jerry— Doctor Kramer," she said. "If you want to wait . . ."

"Do I get to see your office?" he asked lightly. "I could make my call from there."

"Oh. All right. Sure, why not?" But Shelley knew exactly why not. So far the two of them had played out their encounter in public. She couldn't shake the memory of the electricity that had passed between them the first few times their eyes had met. What would that turn into once they were really alone?

Not a thing, she told herself sternly as she opened the door to her office and escorted him in. After all, she was a woman in charge of her own life. It wasn't as if she were prone to irresistible impulses. Far from it.

He walked in slowly, looking about at her office with a practiced eye, letting his attention shift from her desk to her bookcase, to the couch—one after another, as though cataloging the ingredients of her life.

"Casing the joint?" she asked dryly as she moved toward the large oak desk where the telephone sat, square, black, and old-fashioned, the way she liked it.

"Getting a feel for it," he agreed, his voice vaguely absent. She turned to see what had captured his interest and found him staring at a painting on the wall. It was a Mary Cassatt print showing a woman smiling over two playing children, and she watched him take in every line, every shading of color, before he turned his attention away, as though he'd soaked up everything like a sponge and was ready to move on.

"The phone." She held out the receiver, and he walked over to take it from her.

She rummaged in her drawer while he made the call, asking someone to deliver his car. She really didn't need anything there, but she had to do something with her hands while she wondered what she was going to do with him while he waited for his transportation. Her fingers connected with the square tinted glasses she sometimes used when she was reading, and she pulled them out and slid them across her nose.

Good. Just the feel of them on her face would remind her of her professionalism. A small life preserver to cling to, but better than nothing at all.

"Now, then." He hung up the phone and turned to look at her, his gaze bright with anticipation. "Everything's settled. All I need is something to pass the time while I wait for my car to arrive."

"I . . ." This was ridiculous! She was backing away from him as though he were stalking her—a frightened little furry animal hoping to elude the jungle cat. "Would you like to go over and meet Jerry? I'm sure he'd be—"

"No." He moved purposefully toward her, stopping just a foot away. "No, I have a better idea."

She stared up into his eyes, wary of what his "better idea" might be. Suddenly his blue eyes seemed to have limitless depths, as though she'd stepped off reality into a misty world of pure emotion. She opened her mouth, but no sound came out. Was he going to kiss her? She knew she wouldn't turn him away.

But he didn't kiss her. Instead, he took her hand and began to lead her over to the overstuffed, leather couch. "I've never been analyzed before," he told her with what seemed like candid seriousness. "Show me how it's done. Let me know what to expect." He grinned as he gave her a little push that landed her on the cushion. "After all, you're dressed for the part now. Why not go all the way and play the role?"

He was talking about her glasses. She shoved them back on her nose with a mixture of defiance and desperation. She felt like a fool. Had he guessed that she'd expected a kiss? If so, why hadn't he gone ahead and done it?

Well, he could forget it now! She'd be damned if she'd ever kiss him.

"Why not?" she managed to say almost crisply. "But we can't sit together on the couch to do that. I'll have to sit in the chair."

"Are you kidding?" He dropped down beside her. "I can't shout across that gulf. I can get much more intimate right here next to you."

She opened her mouth to protest, then snapped it shut again. She wasn't about to make things worse by letting him know how much it disturbed her to sit so close to him. "I'll need my notebook," she said instead, and he reached across to the desk and handed it to her, along with a pen.

"I'll be a model subject," he told her, leaning back and gazing at her. "Bring on your bizarre experiments, your naked encounter groups, your primal scream therapy. I'm ready for anything."

Smothering a smile, she tried to look severe. "Those are all forms of behavior therapy, meant to deal with symptoms. That's not what we do here. We believe in psychoanalysis—looking into the past, into the subconscious, and into current transactions, for clues to why we act as we do."

He groaned. "Naked encounter groups sound like more fun."

Ignoring that, she tapped her pen against her notebook. If she worked very hard at it, maybe she could actually achieve a sense of professional purpose here, something solid to hold back the dizzy excitement that threatened to creep in and destroy her defenses. "Sit back and relax," she told him as firmly as possible. Surely she could rely on the structures she was familiar with. "Tell me about yourself, about your background. Where did you grow up?"

"Grow up?" He frowned in mock contemplation, and she knew immediately that she might as well head for the trenches. Professional distance wasn't going to help her now. "Let me think. It's kind of hard to remember. The answer seems to be shrouded in the mists of time."

She watched skeptically as he moved closer to her on the couch. What now? Should she call his bluff or wait and see where it led? As if she didn't know exactly where he was heading!

"Maybe if we tried a little relaxation exercise," he suggested, his voice low and seductive. "I'm sure it would all come back to me."

It was time to leap up and insist he leave, to talk about how much work she had waiting on her desk, to tell him how nice it had been to spend the afternoon with him--but don't call us, we'll call you. She'd done that often before. She'd become as adept at brushing off men as she had door-to-door salesmen. Why did it seem to be impossible to do the same to this man, so obviously on the prowl?

His arm was definitely behind her shoulders now, and he was sitting much too close. And here she was, actually smiling up into his face! Was she out of her mind?

She struggled to come out of the spell, but it was hopeless. The sense of his masculine appeal was wafting about her in a sensual cloud. She felt almost drugged by his closeness.

"Anything to help you regain your memory," she heard herself saying breathlessly, and a part of her recoiled in horror. But the rest of her was floating on a cloud.

He was so close now, she could close her eyes and feel the imprint of him without sight. The vibrations of his voice tickled her earlobe. Suddenly he had her chin in his fingers, and the other hand resting behind her shoulder rose and sank into her thick hair, holding her head. "I think it's all coming back," he murmured. "But let's not stop now. We want to make sure we do a thorough job of it."

He plucked her glasses from her nose and held her still before him while his mouth lowered to take possession of hers.

Later Shelley decided she must have been hypnotized, put into a trance by the sound of his low voice, the rich masculine scent of his body, the nearness of his solid flesh. There was just no other explanation. Why else would she have let him kiss her the way she did, with no resistance, no struggle?

His lips brushed hers softly at first, then came again more firmly. His warm tongue slipped along the line between her lips, working slowly, insistently, to part them, and then he was inside, letting his tongue fill her, explore her, devour her, turning her blood to a river of heat.

The notebook and pen clattered to the floor, unheeded. Her hands moved, but only to curl around the lapels of his suit coat, as though to hold him to her. His long fingers cupped her cheek, sliding back to thread into her hair, then lower, curving about her slender neck, moving down to the collar of her sweater, gliding beneath the fabric to caress the jutting collarbone and touch the throbbing pulse at the base of her throat.

A strange thing was happening to Shelley. It was as though a door had opened in her mind, a light had switched on, revealing something she'd never really known. She'd never really understood the chemical reaction that could suddenly take place between a man and a woman. Secretly she'd rather thought it must be something made up by overactive imaginations. For all her psychological training she had a hard time believing in the sort of sexual attraction that made a man and a woman cling together as though their lives depended upon it; a compulsion beyond reason, beyond will.

But suddenly she understood it only too well.

Her thought processes faded, the room faded, the world faded, and she was nothing but woman, he was nothing but man. Her hands slid in to touch the warmth of his chest beneath the suit coat, and her mouth moved against his with an urgency born of new discovery. A sighing moan escaped from her throat, low as a cat's purr, elemental as hunger. Every place where her body touched his was sizzling with a golden fire that turned her inside out, like an exotic flower opening to capture the unwitting victim. Shelley Pride was learning more about her own femininity in this one thrilling kiss than she'd learned in a lifetime of living.

She felt him draw back, and she looked blearily

up into his face, vaguely realizing he was looking surprised, as though the intensity of her response had caught him unprepared. But his hesitation only lasted an instant, and she sighed contentedly as he came to her again, curling into his embrace as though she'd found a home there.

He kissed her again, and she kissed him back, caught on the arc of a rainbow of delight. She felt his hand slide beneath the rough material of her sweater to explore the taut flesh over her rib cage, and she stretched beneath it. As he peeled away the cloth and touched her skin a moan rose like a soft growl in her throat, and she found her own hands pulling away the tails of his shirt, reaching for the excitement of the hard, muscular expanse of his torso.

Her sensitive palm slid across his flat stomach, cupping his navel, her fingers arching through the crisp dark hairs that circled it. She felt a shudder ripple through him that sent a wave of excitement crashing into her system. Spreading her hand further, she trembled at the heat.

His mouth was moving on hers, devouring her, and she felt his hand cup the full roundness of her breast, his fingers rubbing the growing tip through the wool with a building urgency.

She'd forgotten who she was, who he was. That no longer mattered. She'd stumbled upon a treasure that she didn't want to release. In some dim recess of her mind she must have heard the door to the office opening, but she didn't let the noise sink into her consciousness. It wasn't until she heard the sharp gasp from her secretary that she reluctantly pulled away from Michael's embrace, and then her first impulse was annoyance at the interruption.

She looked at the secretary's face as the poor woman backed out of the room, her mouth slack with surprise, her eyes wide. Suddenly reality began to flow back, and the golden haze she'd moved in for the last few moments evaporated. The closing of the office door jarred her fully awake. What had she let happen here?

She sprang up from the couch, reaching for her glasses, which Michael had left on the pillow beside him. Jamming them back on her nose as though they would somehow help protect her, she hastily pulled her clothes together and put her hands on her hips, glaring down at the man who still sat casually, a slight smile curving his lips, a mischievous gleam in his blue eyes.

She was trembling and she knew it wasn't with anger, but she had to pretend it was, for without anger she had no defense at all.

"I think you'd better go," she ordered, voice shaking.

He rose slowly, standing tall compared to her medium height. He moved toward her, and she swung away as though to avoid getting burned. "Does this mean I'm fired as your patient?" His voice was tinged with disappointment, but laughter was curling the edges, and she wondered, sick with embarrassment, if he was laughing at her.

She walked quickly to stand beside her massive oak desk in the far corner of the room. "You weren't my patient in the first place," she reminded him evenly. How had she let this happen? She who was always so cool, so composed? Maria must be totally shocked. Oh, well. That part hardly mattered.

But her own peace of mind did. How had she let herself fall under the spell of a man who had told her from the first that lack of commitment was part of his business? If she could chalk it up to experience and forget it, maybe she could get her emotions back to normal. "Thanks for lunch. Stop by at the reception desk and Maria will give you an appointment with Doctor Kramer."

His eyes caught hers and she had to look away again. He was coming closer; slowly, deliberately. She felt panic rise in her throat.

"How about dinner?" he asked softly, his voice slightly puzzled.

She shook her head without looking at him. "I'm afraid I'm busy," she said crisply.

"Shelley, what's the matter?" He tried to reach for her, but she pulled away and took a quick step that put the desk between them.

"Not a thing," she managed to sing out breezily. "But I've got a pile of work here. So if you don't mind . . ." She forced herself to raise her eyes to his. It took all her strength to fight the contagion of his smiling eyes. "Good luck with your life of crime."

He stared into her face for a long, breathless moment, and then shrugged. "Thanks. And happy analyzing to you, Shelley Pride."

He sauntered to the door and pulled it open. Stepping into the doorway, he turned back to salute her with one last wink. Then he was gone.

Shelley sat on the edge of her couch, trying to keep her mind on her patient's lament and her eyes off the clock. It was half past three on Thursday and she knew Michael Harper was in the office across the hall at that very moment, having a session with Jerry Kramer.

It had been two days since the afternoon he'd come into her life and turned it upside down. Two long, soul-searching days during which she'd had plenty of time to go over the scene that had been played out in her office, plenty of time to concoct a whole series of *if-only-I'd-said*'s and *why-*

didn't-I's, but not quite enough time to put him out of her mind.

Her patient, Bob Corbett, was deathly afraid of women, which made it rather ironic that he preferred Shelley to Jerry as a therapist. Bob had been coming to her for almost a year now, and he was still trying to work out the roots of his problem.

"I was telling you about my aunt," he said, "the one who lived with us and kept tarantulas under her bed."

She nodded. Even though she'd heard the tarantula story at least ten times, it wasn't fair of her not to pay close attention to Bob's latest version of it.

"She had these two, they would play, just like a pair of puppies, rolling and tussling. . . ."

Her patient paused, and she allowed her mind to wander to Michael Harper. She could make up an excuse and drop into Jerry's office just before Michael's hour was up. She could pretend she hadn't known he would be there, pretend she had something vital to say to Jerry.

Bob spoke again and she dragged her attention back to him. "Sometimes she put the biggest tarantula on her arm and walked around the house stroking its little back, whispering to it. If she was mad at my mother, she would give it little orders about how it should crawl into Mom's room in the night. She had a birthday party for one of them once. We all had to come and put on paper hats and sing to it. She wanted us to eat a cake she made for it. She used flies instead of raisins."

Shelly restrained a shudder and glanced at the clock. Bob's hour was drawing to an end. She had to bring the session to a close. "Then," she said, "you knew you had to do something, right?"

"Right! I went in with a shoe box and stole every

one of her hairy spiders. I hid them under my bed. I knew she wouldn't come into my room after them." He paused, shaking his head. "She knew my snakes would get her if she tried it."

"Bob." She stood, smoothing out her skirt. "Your time is up now. We'll continue this next week."

He blinked at her, his watery blue eyes placid. "Same time next week?"

"Of course. Confirm the appointment with Maria before you leave. Okay?" She smiled at him.

He ducked his head and made for the door. He could handle anger and disdain, but friendliness made him very uncomfortable.

Now what, Shelley Pride? she asked herself, standing in the middle of her office, undecided. You're not really going to go chasing into Jerry's office. You couldn't be that silly, that blatant.

No, she realized, suddenly sagging. She couldn't. It wasn't in her to throw herself at a man. She'd never done it. She never would. She wasn't even sure why she thought she might want to do it now.

Michael Harper had excited her as no other man had ever done. He'd infuriated her, but he'd also opened a new world to her, a world she'd only glimpsed when he was with her.

A world better left untouched, she added, scolding herself. She sank back down on her couch, holding her arms tightly about her as though to ward off unwelcome feelings.

She'd always felt so smug, so sure no man would ever drag her heart around. She'd seen her friends go through the heartache, and she'd thought her experience with Barry had been her inoculation against the disease. But here she was, letting Michael infect her mind.

Restlessly she rose and paced her office. Love. Who needed it? She'd seen the hunger for it destroy her beautiful mother. She'd been a woman who counted on her looks to pay her way, and when those looks began to fade, she'd retreated into a dreamworld of another time, another place.

It had been her mother's schizophrenia that had interested Shelley in psychology. At first everyone in the family had tried to ignore it, hoping that it would go away if they pretended it already had.

When her mother came down to dinner one night and announced airily that she'd been murdered during her afternoon nap, and this was really her ghost that they saw before them, Shelley knew she had to do something.

She began haunting libraries, reading everything she could on every kind of mental disturbance. With what she learned she began to realize that there was help for her mother, and slowly she convinced the rest of the family to find professional guidance.

But by the time that happened, her mother's misery had lasted for many years, and Shelley was still bitter that she'd had to suffer so long without help. If only they'd known more, understood better. . . . Now her life was devoted to making sure others got the sort of help they needed right from the start.

All in all, she'd been satisfied with her life. She had her friends, her work. She didn't need anything else. But one afternoon with Michael Harper had threatened the structure of her life-style, and she hadn't been the same since.

She really should put these wild ideas out of her head, she told herself. Maybe she should get away for a while. Perhaps she would agree to join Carrie on her vacation at the beach after all. Anything to keep the temptation of Michael from overwhelming her.

Her telephone buzzed, and she stepped to her desk to answer it.

"Doctor Kramer would like to see you right away," Maria said.

Shelley's heart leaped in her throat. "I'll be right out," she answered. She didn't give herself time to think. Speeding out the door of her office into the lobby, she just caught sight of Michael's back as he left the building, stepping out into the parking lot. His black hair shone in the sunlight for just a second, then disappeared from sight.

She stood staring at the swinging door as it came slowly to a stop, her pulse racing, a lump in her throat. He was gone. She wasn't sure if she was disappointed or terribly relieved.

"Shelley?" Jerry was standing in the open door to his office. "Coming to see me?"

A sideways glance found Maria watching her with open interest, and Shelley managed a bright smile for the secretary. "Yes—yes, I am," she told her colleague, and walked on into his room. "Maria said you had something to say to me."

Jerry nodded, pointing out a chair at the far side of his desk for her to sit in. Jerry Kramer was in his mid-thirties, a dark-haired man of medium build. He and Shelley worked well together except when he was between girlfriends. Then he'd say there was "something between the two of them that should be explored." And since he lived in her apartment building, he was sometimes a little difficult to shake off.

"Shelley," he would say, shaking his head sadly, "you don't know what you're missing. We could be so good together."

The thought wasn't even mildly tempting. Jerry was a swinger who bragged about his dates and loved to appear in fancy places with famous names. Shelley could never figure out why he was remotely interested in her, and she said so every time he asked her out.

Jerry never had an answer, but Carrie thought

she knew what it was. "It's your shy, virginal quality," she told Shelley. "It intrigues him."

"Shy! I'm not a bit shy and he knows it!"

Carrie had cocked her head to the side, considering. "No, you're not shy," she conceded. "But your femininity is."

Today Jerry wanted only to get down to business. "I've just seen this Michael Harper character. I know you met him earlier this week. What did you think of him?"

If only she knew. She stifled a smile and shook her head. "I won't be much help to you, Jerry. I . . . didn't really get a fix on him." She took a deep breath. "I imagine he'd be difficult to open up."

"Yeah. These undercover guys are slick operators. They live on deception and they get so good at it, they don't know what reality is anymore."

"Undercover?" She hadn't realized he would tell Jerry about that. But of course, Jerry would know. It was because he worked with the police that they'd picked him as the analyst to help keep the cover alive.

"Sure. Didn't you know? He runs sting operations on con artists. He busted a big ring of mining swindlers in Reno a few years ago. He goes in like he's a rich hick, ripe for the plucking, then he nails the crooks in the middle of their game." Jerry frowned. "I really don't appreciate the department getting me involved this way. Setting up phony appointments. I've got real work to do. I don't have time for this." He shot her a furtive look. "So that's why I'm going to hand him over to you."

"Me?" Her voice came out a piercing squeak. It was impossible. But how could she get out of it?

Very simple, Shelley Pride, she told herself sternly. You just say no.

When she'd first started working with Jerry, three years before, she'd been so grateful to be hired, so eager to please, that she'd done any job he suggested without a murmur of protest. Over the years he got quite used to slipping all the dirty work her way. She'd known for quite a while that it was high time she made a stand. This seemed like a ready-made opportunity to show Jerry she wasn't going to put up with it any longer.

"No way, Jerry." Shaking her head almost violently, she began to back away from his desk. "You're the certified therapist."

He came toward her, brow furrowed. "But you signed for it."

She shook her head, refusing to be bullied. "I signed for you, though, and you know it." She gestured toward the telephone. "Call the department if you want to get out of it. But don't throw him in my lap."

"Thanks a lot," Jerry grumbled, giving it up. "Just remember next time you want a favor from me."

She grinned at him, surprised it had been so easy. "I'll remember." She slipped out of his office and stopped, feeling pleased with herself. Not only had she stood up to Jerry, she'd strengthened her resolve against seeing Michael again. *Good for me*, she thought.

She gave a little dancing two-step in time to the piped-in music and walked across the hall toward her own office. As she passed Maria's desk her glance fell on a book of matches in the ashtray. "Smoking again, Maria?" she asked teasingly, knowing the secretary fought a perpetual battle with cigarettes.

Maria looked surprised. "What? Oh, no. Those are Mr. Harper's." She shuddered dramatically. "Get them out of here, would you? I hate to be reminded, especially at this time in the afternoon."

Shelley obediently picked up the matches and put them in her pocket.

Back in her office, she pulled them out again and turned them in her fingers. THE BAY VISTA GRAND HOTEL, NEWPORT BEACH. Funny, Shelley thought, that was one of the hotels Carrie had been talking about staying in.

Carrie had been trying to talk her into coming along on a vacation to the nearby beach resort for months. "You need to get away from this constant grind," she'd argued. "You need to kick off your shoes and put on a bikini. Be a woman for a change!"

And behind that, of course, Carrie meant be a woman and find a man. She knew her friend worried about her. Carrie had been her roommate in college, and they'd moved in together again only a few months before when Carrie had separated from her husband of five years. He was on an engineering assignment in South America, but the split had come about more because of marital problems than because of job situations. Carrie made no bones about needing a man in her life.

Shelley's fingers tightened on the matchbook cover. Maybe she would go with Carrie after all. The thought sent her pulse racing again.

Was she crazy? Irrationally she began to laugh softly. Yes, yes, she was crazy. That was exactly it. She couldn't get the man out of her mind.

She closed her eyes and leaned back in her swivel chair. She knew he was poison, and yet she also knew that he offered an excitement she wouldn't be able to resist.

Well, never mind, she told herself. He hadn't shown any signs of wanting to see her again. And why should he? Go with Carrie, she told herself, and have a nice vacation. But don't expect to see Michael Harper.

She turned to look at the picture he'd stared at on her wall. Pressing her fingers to her lips, she remembered the kiss they'd shared, and something inside seemed to curl at the memory, tightening so quickly that she gasped.

Four

Carrie was pouting, holding out a slick brown object on a fork. "Just one more chocolate-covered strawberry. Come on, I'll share it with you."

Shelley groaned, leaning back in her velvet padded chair. "Not another bite. Really, I'll blow up like a blimp and float off if I do. I haven't eaten this much since the Thanksgiving when I was ten."

All the restaurants in the Bay Vista Grand served wonderful food, but the Boar's Head, where they were dining on this Saturday night, was especially nice.

"That veal was as tender as fish, honestly. And that caper sauce . . ." Carrie swooned back in her seat, ecstasy written all over her pretty face. Shelley's roommate shared her type of build, but for some reason it looked very different on her. She'd been an athlete in school, always out for the track team or playing basketball, and it still showed in her bearing and casual manner.

"Yes," Shelley agreed. "Everything was marvelous. Everything except those slimy snails. Why you always have to order those things, I can't understand." Shelley shuddered.

"It could be worse," Carrie answered. "Just think of what a meal would be like with that patient of yours, the tarantula-spider guy."

Shelley laughed. Though she never referred to her patients by name, she sometimes told Carrie anecdotes about her day. She'd almost told her about Michael Harper the night after she'd met him, but something held her back. Even now, as her gaze quickly skimmed the tables of the large dining room, looking for a sign of him, she hadn't told her roommate why she'd agreed to come on this vacation with her, and why she'd insisted upon the Bay Vista Grand.

They'd arrived late Friday afternoon and had joined the other guests at the TGIF cocktail party around the outdoor fountains. They'd dined in the Boar's Head, then gone on to spend a few hours in the disco downstairs. Carrie had found a man as athletic as she, and the two of them had danced continuously, while Shelley had turned down more suitors than she'd obliged with a dance, growing progressively more and more exhausted by the effort her friend seemed to be putting out.

They'd slept, spent Saturday sailing, playing tennis, and walking the length of Balboa Island before showering and dressing for dinner at the Boar's Head.

Michael Harper had never appeared. When she thought about it now, Shelley had to smile at her own adolescent behavior. Of course, he wasn't here. For all she knew, he'd picked up the matchbook cover in a bar in Timbuktu. Why she'd been compelled to come here she wasn't sure. It was ridiculous, and she was glad now that she hadn't told Carrie the truth.

No, he wasn't here. And yet she'd still dressed as though she hoped to see—well, someone special. She'd borrowed another dress from Carrie, a light chiffon in rainbow colors that was tight across the bodice and swirled around her legs as she walked.

"We've got to find you a man," Carrie was saying now, sprawling across her chair like a friendly puppy. "I mean, what did we come for anyway?"

Shelley smiled at her friend. "I came for a little relaxation and a little fun, to get my head out of my psychology texts and see what the rest of the world's been up to while I've been drowning myself in case studies and personality evaluations. Why did you come?"

Carrie grinned. She was not to be dissuaded from her path. "To find *you* a man. And look what happened. I was the one who ended up doing all the dancing last night." She shook her head sternly. "No, tonight we find one for you."

"Oh, Carrie," she moaned. "I'm so full, I don't think I can walk, much less dance. Let's pass on that tonight."

"Not on your life. If we don't get busy, we'll end up leaving before we have anything to show for this whole vacation."

"I've got a start on this summer's tan," she answered hopefully. "Won't that count?"

They paused while the waiter refilled their coffee cups.

"No more for me," Carrie said. "I want to run up and change my shoes. This pair is killing me. I'll never be able to dance in them. I'll meet you back down here in a few minutes."

Carrie hurried off while Shelley sat alone at her table, watching the other diners. A couple across the room was obviously in love. She wondered if this was their honeymoon. Something about the way they sat—so close together, their heads almost touching—pulled at her heart, making it twist painfully in her chest.

The time sped by and Carrie didn't reappear, so Shelley decided to go on up and meet her at the room. She signed the check, gathered her purse, and threaded her way out between the tables into the lobby. As she was leaving the huge room she looked back for one last scan across the assembly, and as she did, she ran into someone coming in around the corner.

She knew who he was before her head had swung around. Every nerve end was jangling, every sense aware.

"Michael!"

He stared down at her, his brows pulled together in consternation, holding her back from the collision they'd just had. "Oh, Michael." For some reason she was laughing, probably from pure embarrassment.

"Who's this, Mike?" The couple coming in behind him came into her field of vision for the first time. "Someone from home?"

She looked back up into his face, startled to see him mouthing something to her he obviously didn't want the others to hear, but she hadn't caught enough of it to know what he was trying to convey to her.

"Julie, darling," he said aloud, quickly wrapping his arms about her and pulling her close. "What a surprise."

She gasped at the strength of his hug, struggling against it, but at the same time she heard his whisper in her ear: "Just follow my lead."

He planted a loud smack on her mouth and pulled away, still holding her with one tight arm about her shoulders while she reeled from the unexpected contact.

"It's Julie. She's flown out from Tulsa to surprise me." He motioned toward the other two. "Julie, meet a wonderful couple, Clayton and Margery Weeks. This here's my wonderful little wife, Julie Daniels."

Wife? She gazed from one face to the other, completely at sea, but not sure what to do about it. If this was a joke, she might as well let it ride until she got the punchline.

"How—how do you do?" She put out a tentative hand that was overwhelmed by Mr. Weeks's elegantly long fingers, then by the shorter but no less elegant hand of his wife. The two of them looked like an ad for a very expensive automobile. Except for the American accent, she wouldn't have been surprised to hear them announced as the lord and lady of some British title.

Michael was dressed in slacks and a plaid sports coat, a style at odds with the fashionable dress she'd seen him in before. But somehow it looked just as natural. She had a feeling he would look at home in any outfit. He seemed to take on the characteristics he needed along with the clothes.

"Julie, honey, I can't believe it! What did you do with the kids? Who's looking after my tomato plants?" He grinned at the Weekses. "Only about six inches high, but already they're putting out buds. Amazing. We'll have tomatoes by Memorial Day, guaranteed."

Shelley felt as though her head were spinning, as though she'd stepped into some sort of time warp. She didn't dare look the Weekses in the eye, so she kept her gaze trained almost desperately on Michael, hoping to learn what on earth was going on. But the truth was slowly seeping in on her. There was only one explanation possible. She'd obviously walked into the middle of Michael Harper at work. Of course, that was what it was. He was in the middle of one of his undercover operations, and she'd blundered into it.

"Your table, Mr. Weeks."

The Weekses were an impressive-looking couple. She noticed they rated the manager as their escort. Whatever, they were Michael's business. The sooner she faded from the scene, the better he would probably like it. Smiling warily, she began backing away. "I really have to go. . . ."

"You're just in time for dinner, Julie," Michael told her heartily, stopping her retreat as he tightened the arm that held her. "Just wait till you taste the food here. We've got nothing like this in Tulsa."

The thought of eating again sent a sick shudder through her. "Oh, no," she said, trying to smile. "Why don't I just—"

"You ate on the plane from Tulsa, did you?" Michael's grin was mildly wicked. She found herself smiling back, caught up in his charm once again. "Never mind. You'll forget all that when you see the menu here."

"I've seen the menu here," she managed to hiss as they walked behind the Weekses toward their table. Michael was still holding her, and she couldn't help but notice how nicely they fitted together. "I feel as though I've eaten everything on it tonight."

"You're doing great," he whispered back, ignoring her complaint. "Just keep it up for another hour or so. That's all I ask." He hugged her close for a quick kiss on the cheek as the other couple turned to face them.

"Really, honey," he said more loudly, "I've missed you so much. Just ask the Weekses. Why, I haven't been able to stop talking about you."

Shelley wondered if this was what it would be like to be Michael Harper's wife. It felt rather warm and wonderful so far. But then she realized her mistake. She wasn't playing Michael's wife at all. She was Mrs. Mike Daniels.

The Weekses' table was out on the glass-enclosed balcony that afforded a stunning view of the bay in twilight as the yachts were coming in to their moorings. The setting sun turned the sea to molten gold while the sky was stained with glowing amber.

Mr. Weeks was smiling at her as they sat down at the round boothlike table. Michael slid in beside her, the length of his hard thigh pressed tightly against hers. Despite the strangeness of this encounter, she felt an exotic excitement at his touch, at the sense of the maleness in him. She found herself smiling at him almost shyly, enjoying the sparkle in his blue eyes.

"Mrs. Daniels—do you mind if I call you Julie?" Clayton Weeks asked. "Julie, we're so glad you could make it out here to the coast. We've been telling your husband here for days that we wanted you to see the property too. We always like to get the wife in on the deal right from the beginning."

Shelley tried to smile, hoping they would take her discomfort for the natural reserve of a stranger unused to the setting and the company and not the total confusion of an impostor. She sat silently while the others ordered wine and talked about the property Michael seemed to be thinking of buying from the Weekses.

Not five minutes before she'd been sitting all alone at a table, vaguely hoping to catch a glimpse of Michael, but planning to get up to her room and go to bed with a good book within the hour. Now here she was, playing the part of Michael's wife. She still hadn't got her bearings. Just what did Michael expect her to do here anyway?

Suddenly her eyes connected with Carrie's. Her friend was standing a few tables away behind the Weekses' backs. As Shelley looked up she saw Carrie grin and flash her an okay sign with thumb to forefinger. She'd obviously seen Michael and thought Shelley had caught herself a willing victim at last. Just as obviously, she approved.

There was no way to send a distress signal. And anyway, Shelley wasn't sure she would have if she could. Watching Carrie stroll away, she knew she was stranded for the duration.

Margery Weeks was gazing at her with a studied air. "I'm so glad you could leave the children. How many did Mike say you have?"

Margery's eyes were guileless, but Shelley had a sudden intuition that she was being tested nonetheless. She hesitated, hoping Michael would answer for her, but instead, she suddenly felt his hand on her leg, just above the knee, and his fingers were tapping out the number—one, two, three.

"The children?" Margery asked a little more sharply.

"Oh." Shelley laughed nervously to cover her pause. "Three, of course. You'll have to excuse me. I think I've got jet lag."

She smiled at Michael, then put a dagger in it to let him know it was now time for him to take his hand back off her leg, but he merely grinned back.

His warmth penetrated the thin chiffon in no time, and she felt it spreading across her skin, teasing the tiny hairs and sending chills up her thigh. This had to stop. He had no right to hold her there. She tried to move her leg, but his grip was too strong.

She picked up her wineglass as soon as the wine steward filled it and held it up to the light, watching the glow of the candlelight filter through the golden liquid, but sensitive only to the hand that was still resting on her flesh. Michael was walking a thin edge and he must know that. She was getting angry, and she was quite capable of blowing his whole operation right here and now. She threw him another glance that said exactly that and he read it clearly, but his fingers tightened on her leg, moving softly, his palm caressing her through the flimsy material.

She dropped one hand as though to hold the napkin in her lap, but instead, it went right to the intruder and began to try to pry his fingers off, one by one, while she smiled inanely at the other couple.

"Three children," Margery went on as the wine steward left them. "They must keep you busy. Did Michael tell us they were all boys?"

"Yes," was on the top of her tongue, but a sudden fierce grip on her leg stopped her.

"No, no," Michael said cheerfully. "All girls. I call them my little harem."

Shelley winced.

"And the oldest is seven?"

This time his fingers tightened once, twice, in a clear signal. "Yes," he answered. "And the others are three and four, aren't they darling?" The double signal came again.

Ah-hah, she thought, suddenly realizing his purpose. Once means no, twice means yes. She stopped prying and let her hand rest on her napkin instead. His hand began to move caressingly again, as though to erase the harshness of his grip. The chiffon seemed to melt away, leaving only the silky nothing of her nylons between his hands and the sensitive flesh of her inner thigh.

"That's right," she said, meeting Michael's blue eyes with a look that was half defiant, half pleading. "And every one is spoiled rotten by her daddy." All of a sudden she began to enjoy her role. As long as she was in this thing, why not play it to the hilt? If only Michael's hand on her leg didn't destroy her ability to cope.

"You and Mike seem like a loving couple," Margery said approvingly. "You could almost pass for honeymooners."

"Oh, yes," Shelley answered quickly, remembering to soften the edges of her speech just a touch in hopes of mimicking the Oklahoma drawl in passable fashion. She'd noticed Michael was doing just that from the first. "Why, Mike and I are so lovey-dovey, we embarrass the neighbors back home in Tulsa. I've had ladies on our block ask if we couldn't please keep the shades down. They told me it was making them downright jealous. You see, none of them have husbands with as much"— she poked Michael with an exaggerated elbow thrust—"get up and go as Mike. If you know what I mean."

The Weekses looked as though someone had just poured dirty dishwater in their soup bowls, and Michael's smile was strained. His fingers were drumming an irritated beat on the inside of her leg. Shelley sat grinning ingenuously while the others picked up their huge menus and held them before their faces.

"Don't overdo it," Michael whispered to her behind his.

"Why not?" she whispered back. "It's so much fun." She leaned close as though to kiss his cheek. "And you deserve it," she told him sweetly.

Suddenly his face had turned and his mouth was on hers, kissing her for real. "I've missed you, Julie," he said in a loud whisper meant to be heard by all. "Let's get this dinner over with and get back to the room."

She drew back, shocked, then had to laugh as she saw the devil in his eyes. What was he doing, after all, but filling out the character she'd set for him?

But she knew it couldn't go on. If they weren't careful, they'd sabotage Michael's operation with their own little battle. She settled back and determined to be more circumspect.

Watching Michael at work was an education in itself. He was every bit the hearty, good-natured midwestern man, lovable and seemingly all gullibility. No one could help but like him, and yet he was making himself out to be a first-rate victim.

She could fairly see the Weekses' eyes gleam as he spoke of all the money he'd supposedly made on his cousin's oil venture in Oklahoma, and how he wanted to find just the right thing to invest it in.

At first she'd found it hard to believe such cultured people could be crooks, but as she watched and listened, she began to see it. They thought they had a prime pigeon here, fat and ready for plucking, no doubt about it. She enjoyed knowing they were busy digging their own graves.

Michael's hand stayed on her leg, signaling whenever questions put her on the spot. She had to admit it felt perfectly marvelous there, close and warm and thrilling. The sensation it created made her want to cuddle in against him and reach inside his shirt to find a piece of his warmth for her own. If it sometimes seemed to be moving a little too high, his thumb stroking a little too close, that only added another element of excitement.

She almost groaned aloud when the main course was served. She'd tried to order the lightest thing on the menu, poached salmon, but when it came drizzled with dill cucumber sauce and ensconced in decorative swirls of duchess potatoes, she knew she was in trouble.

The chocolate-covered strawberries were haunting her as she stared the salmon down. How could she possibly take a bite? Maybe she could push it around on her plate until the others would finish and no one would notice. . . .

"Come on, Julie," Michael said with hearty spirit. "Eat up. You're going to need your strength tonight."

Throwing him a baleful glance, she took one bite, then another. It became an automatic thing, and not too painful as long as she kept her mind off what she was doing. By the time the waiter served the demitasse cups, she felt rather like a salmon herself, one that had been tossed up on the deck and was gasping for air.

"We're going to have to call it a night early," Michael told the Weekses. "You can see how tired Julie is."

Shelley looked at him gratefully. "Yes, I am that," she agreed. "I need a good night's sleep."

"That's fine with us," Clayton Weeks piped in. "We like to turn in early ourselves. And we'll want to get an early start to take you out to that property tomorrow."

"Oh . . ." Shelley thought fast. "I'm afraid that will be impossible. You see, I only ran out here on the spur of the moment to see my little Mikey." She reached up and pinched his cheek. "I have to go back first thing in the morning."

"What time is your flight?"

"Early," she answered hastily. "Very, very early."

"No problem," Margery told her. "I'm always up at four myself. I do calisthenics for an hour, then yoga for another hour and a half. I'll drop by your room and pick you up. We can stop by the property on the way to the airport."

Shelley looked questioningly at Michael, sure that he would come up with a way out of this. Surely he didn't expect her to rejoin this group in the morning! But Michael was smiling witlessly at them all, as though he hadn't a care in the world.

They rose and left the dining room, Michael holding firmly to her shoulders. The Weekses escorted them up to Michael's room, and Shelley began to wonder if they had suspicions. What were they planning to do, come right into the room to watch the Danielses get ready for bed? This could go right beyond embarrassing on into humiliation. But helpless as she was to do anything else, she followed along feeling comfortable, yet wary, in the curve of Michael's arm.

"Good night, you two," Margery Weeks told them at the doorway, bringing a sigh of relief to Shelley's lips. "Now, don't forget, first thing in the morning. I'll give you a little knock like this." She demonstrated, while Michael and Shelley stood in the open door, smiling and waiting to be left alone.

"Good night!"

"Good night!"

The older couple turned the corner, and the two of them collapsed back into the room, rolling with laughter.

Michael held her to him as they laughed, and she let him, totally consumed with mirth over the events of the evening.

"I can't believe that you put me through this," she gasped, wiping the tears from her eyes. "I've never spent such an absolutely nerve-racking night before in my life."

He chuckled, holding her away a bit so that he could look down into her eyes. "But you enjoyed every minute, didn't you?" he accused.

To her surprise she realized he was right. "Yes," she admitted. "I guess I did." She grinned. "What a tacky couple we Danielses are."

The shadow of a frown passed over his face. "In retrospect that might have been a bit unfortunate," he said slowly. "The real Danielses are great people. I hate to do that to their reputations."

She blinked up at him. "Do you mean to tell me there really is a Daniels family from Tulsa?"

He nodded. "Mike and Julie. Absolutely. People like the Weekses check these things out."

She began to notice the setting around them. They were in Michael's hotel room. The bed was huge, dominating the area, and suddenly the adventure fantasy they'd been living in for the last two hours faded, leaving only stark reality.

She pulled out of his arms, embarrassed to be clinging to him still, and backed toward the door.

"Nice room you have here," she said, trying to keep her tone light and breezy. "Much swankier than the one I'm sharing with Carrie—my room-mate," she added in quick explanation.

She licked her lips as she watched Michael turn back the downy covers of the huge bed.

"Look comfortable enough to you?" he asked, humor glinting in his blue eyes.

"Uh . . . I think . . ." She looked over her shoulder for the doorway, then looked back to find Michael shrugging out of his jacket and reaching for the knot in his tie.

"You don't want to go," he said quietly. "What will the Weekses think?"

The tie came off and landed on top of the jacket, which he'd slung across a handy chair. He unbuttoned the top two buttons of his shirt and started on the third, taking another step toward her with each button he released.

"They must be out of range by now," she said, her voice low with wary unease. "I'll get on back to my own room."

He shook his head, his eyes narrowed as he came closer, steadily, smoothly, like a panther stalking his prey. "No, you don't, Shelley," he said softly. "You're staying here tonight."

Her hand went unconsciously to her throat as she found herself backed against the door. "I'm not either," she said unsteadily. "No way."

He came up against her, leaning against the door with one hand on either side of her head, trapping her. "Oh, yes, you are," he said huskily. "We have some unfinished business, you and I."

She had to try twice before she could get a word out. "I don't know what you're talking about," she protested at last.

"Don't you?" He leaned down and planted one

firm kiss on her trembling mouth. "Don't you remember what happened in your office the other day?"

She tried to shake her head in the negative, but he laughed softly. "I remember it. In fact, I haven't been able to get it out of my head for days." He dropped another kiss on her lips, branding them with a flame as potent as a shot of cognac. "I've never seen a woman turn from ice to fire in such a short time, Shelley. You surprised me. You opened a door I didn't expect. And now I mean to take advantage of that invitation."

Five

"Michael!" She meant to snap the name out as a reprimand, but somehow it came out a like sighing caress instead. "Oh, Michael."

His face was nuzzling into the curve of her neck and she felt his breath on her skin, hot and tantalizing. "Invite me again, Shelley," he murmured. "Only this time don't pull the door closed at the last minute."

His large hands were sliding down her back, curving around the fullness of her hips, pulling her gently against his body so that she could feel just what he was talking about, and her senses swirled in confusion. "Michael. . . ."

Why couldn't she get any further than his name? She felt like a fool, knowing on one level that he was seducing her before her very eyes, so to speak, and that she should tell him firmly that she wanted no part of him, and yet totally unable to get the words out, even to force her hands to try to push him away. It was as though every part of her body were conspiring against her. Was there no one left on her side? And just what was her side anyway?

"There'll be no secretary walking in on us this time, Shelley," he breathed against the skin of her neck. "We'll be all alone, and we'll be able to finish what we start."

He raised his head, gazing into her dark eyes, his hips still pressing hers, holding her still. "What do you say, lady shrink? You ready to mess around with my psyche a little more?"

"A little more?" she managed to force out, avoiding his eyes by looking at the dark wealth of hair that curled up into the opening of his shirt. Talk. That was it. If she could carry on a conversation, maybe she could forget just what was really happening. And if she forgot, she wouldn't have to make any decisions about it, would she? "How did I 'mess around' with your psyche before?"

His chuckle warmed her even more than his body did and she looked up quickly, then found herself laughing back into his eyes. "I think you know the answer to that," he said, his hands circling her waist. "But don't let that stop you." His hands were moving slowly, inexorably higher, rubbing along her rib cage. "Experiment with me all you want."

Why was she laughing? She had no idea what he was talking about, but it seemed so funny anyway. The pressure of his hips against hers was sending electricity through her system, and she didn't want to think about that. Laughing was much better.

But kissing was better still. That was the conclusion she came to as his mouth covered hers again, moving softly, smoothly, deliciously over her lips, then descending into the heat of her mouth, filling her with wonder at the complexities he aroused in her.

How could something feel at once so warm and secure and comforting, and still send her reeling with excitement and danger? It didn't make sense, and yet it was so completely irresistible, she wanted more, more. . . .

His hands were cupping her breasts, shooting a shock wave of desire through her body, and she gasped, pulling back and trying to push away.

"Oh, no, you don't," he informed her soothingly, thrusting his knee between her thighs to help hold her right where she was. "Just like the sushi, we'll take it a step at a time. Trust me."

"I trust you," she replied, but something was very wrong. It was the sushi that finally set it off for her. Suddenly, just the thought of food made pink spots float before her eyes. She leaned back against the door. "I want to lie down," she whispered. Too much wine, too much food. Then he'd said *sushi*, and the room was spinning.

Of course, he misunderstood. "Don't worry," he said sensuously as he ran tiny kisses along the taut line of her neck, kisses that at any other time might have been her undoing. "So do I."

She took a deep breath of air. "Right now," she insisted, stiffening urgently.

Finally he began to get the picture. He drew back, puzzled. "Shall I carry you to the bed?" he asked, not sure yet whether to be alarmed or amused.

"No time," she answered tragically, feeling very green. "I think this nice soft carpet will have to do."

It did very well. As her knees gave way, Michael took over, helping her lie back. She snuggled gratefully into the thick pile. "That's better," she whispered, closing her eyes. "Much, much better."

He was kneeling over her, pushing a pillow under her head, his face a mixture of amusement and concern. "Better than what?" he asked lightly. "Than kissing me?"

"Oh, no." She looked up quickly, wanting to reassure him. "That was very nice too."

"Thanks," he answered wryly. "But do you mind telling me just what the problem is? Surely you didn't have enough wine to—"

"No." She reached for his hand and held it in her own. She felt pretty silly lying on the floor this way, but anything was better than the bed. Somehow she couldn't face that. Not yet. And this was kind of friendly really. Like lying on the grass, exchanging confidences on a warm summer evening. Luckily the carpet was as plush as they came, and very comfortable, considering. "I'm so sorry, Michael. But this really is your fault anyway."

He shook his head in bewilderment. "You're allergic to me?" he guessed. "If so, you're in big trouble." He grimaced. "We're both in big trouble."

"No, that's not it." She smiled up at him. "It's the food." She groaned at the thought of it. "You made me eat two dinners, you know. And my stomach is rebelling."

"Is that all?" He gave a snort of mock disgust. "And here I thought you were tough."

"I am tough," she protested, for no apparent reason. Why should she be tough, after all? What did he think she was doing, applying for a partnership in his dangerous profession? "This has nothing to do with tough. I'd like to see how you looked after two full course dinners in a row."

"I could handle it," he said in his best macho voice.

"Well, I can't." She moaned, closing her eyes again. "I feel like a very large, very unhappy, beached whale."

"That's funny," he replied, reaching out to brush the hair back away from her eyes. "You *look* like a very desirable woman. I guess my mind must be playing tricks on me." He cupped her cheek and said more softly, "Unless you are."

She looked at him again, her eyes wide. "I'm not making this up," she assured him earnestly. "I can't move. Really." She put a hand on her stomach, surprised to find it still relatively flat. The way she felt, it ought to be blown up like a balloon. "You should hear what's going on in here," she told him. "Then you'd see for yourself."

He grinned. "Why not?" And the next thing she knew, his head was on her stomach, ear down. "Good Lord," he said.

"What's the matter?" She craned her head to see him, but he motioned her to be still. His face was intent, as though he were listening to something very interesting.

This was ridiculous. She wanted to laugh, but she was afraid she'd bounce his head right off onto the floor. "What is it?" she asked again, beginning to really wonder.

"Amazing." He grinned at her. "It sounds like a whole nation of busy little workers, all bustling about their little chemical tasks." A look of astonishment crossed his handsome face. "Wait," he said, motioning her to silence again.

This time she couldn't hold back the giggle. "Michael, get off!" she begged. "You're making me laugh, and I'm too stuffed to laugh."

He raised his head, his eyes glowing with humor. "I wish you could hear this one," he said. "Sounds like a basketball game going on in center court. Something's bouncing."

"The chocolate-covered strawberries." She nodded wisely. "I knew they were a mistake from the beginning."

"You see, it wasn't my fault at all." He flopped down next to her on the floor, looking pleased with himself. "It was the first meal you ate that ruined you. Not the second."

"Let's not talk about food." She moaned again. "How am I going to get back to my room?" She looked at him speculatively. "I wonder if they have a cot with wheels? Then you could roll me down the halls . . ."

"You're not rolling anywhere," he informed her firmly. "You're staying right here."

So they were back to that again, Shelley thought. He wanted her to stay the night. Small butterflies of panic winged their way through the other feelings she was being swamped with.

Well, what did you expect, Shelley my dear? she asked herself sarcastically. What else did you come to this resort for? Didn't you hope, deep in your heart, that just this very thing would happen? That you would find Michael and that he would want you?

Funny how easy it had seemed in dreams, and how much more difficult it seemed in reality. But she didn't feel much like laughing about it.

Luckily there was something to hide behind. "You want me to stay, even if I'm like this?" Once he realized how seriously stuffed she really was, surely he wouldn't be able to get her out the door fast enough.

He shrugged. "Like this, or any other way. All of a sudden, I can't imagine the night without you." His grin took away the seriousness of the words. "You're in my blood, lady. You might as well face it."

What on earth was he talking about? "Maybe you'd better tell me just exactly what facing it involves," she said, feeling a little shaky.

He took a moment to answer her question, and she swung around to look at him again. He was lying beside her, very casually propped up on one elbow. His free hand was playing with her hair, twisting it around his fingers in a random pattern.

"I'm afraid I can't answer that question," he said at last, his voice strangely low and lacking any trace of the ironic humor that laced most of his statements. "I don't think I've ever had a woman in my blood before. We'll have to wait and see."

She looked into his blue eyes, searching harder, hoping to see a glint of the joke he must be playing on her. What could he mean? He barely knew her. He couldn't possibly be—

Her mind shrank from continuing along that train of thought, and he helped by saying, "In the meantime we'll have to find a way to fill the time until you feel like your old self. I don't suppose you'd be up to charades?"

She shook her head, smiling at his doubtful look. Of course, he'd been joking. There was no other explanation. She felt a warm blanket of comforting relief settle over their scene.

"I'm afraid singing you love songs is out," he said regretfully. "I can't carry a tune to save my life. One of my few flaws, I might point out." He tugged softly at her hair. "I could rub you all over," he suggested hopefully. "A good massage to get the circulation pumping. Wouldn't that make you feel better?"

She threw him a baleful glare, forcing back the smile that threatened to cover her features. "I doubt it."

"Too bad." He sighed his regret, then his face lit up. "I know," he announced like the man who'd just invented plastic wrap. "What you need is a cathartic experience. Something to get this food business out of your system once and for all."

Shelley raised a skeptical eyebrow. "The goal sounds good," she admitted. "Pardon me if I'm a bit leery of the means."

He shook his head, a triumphant smile lighting his eyes. "No need to be. This is just the thing." He threw back his head proudly. "Food jokes."

She closed her eyes. "Oh, no. . . ."

"You'll love them. Here goes." He cleared his

throat. "Why did the young lettuce cross the road?"

All she could manage was a weak cry of protest. "Michael—"

"Because it was time for him to leaf home."

Her groan echoed from wall to wall in the large bedroom.

Michael put on his best cornball-comedian voice. "Don't worry if you didn't like that one. I've got a hundred more where it came from."

"No!"

His eyes were huge with mock pain. "Shelley, believe me, you've got to learn to laugh at food. Control it before it controls you. It's the only way."

She *was* laughing, she realized, and that made her stomach bounce and that didn't feel good at all, so she rolled over, cradling her head in her folded arms. Her move put her closer to him, and when she looked up again, she found his face only inches from hers. His eyes were a deep, beguiling velvet-blue, the kind of blue that made her want to sink into it and lose herself, sliding down the surface and into the heart of its vibrant color. He stared down at her and she stared up at him, indulging herself, letting her mind go blank, only enjoying the blueness, and then something flickered there, pulling her back alert. She looked sharply, trying to follow the flicker, to find out just exactly what it was, and feeling like Alice chasing the White Rabbit.

"We could always tell ghost stories," Michael said softly, his hand suddenly stroking her hair, as if to distract her from what she'd seen in his eyes. "Or I could tie a love knot from your beautiful hair."

Her heart was beating so hard, Shelley knew he had to hear it. She wasn't sure what had set it off. It could be that her senses were noticing something she hadn't seen herself. Was it a warning? Or anticipation? "Do you know how to tie a love knot?" she asked, more to keep the conversation flowing than to find an answer to her question.

"No." His eyes were shaded from her now. He was examining her hair, taking it up in his fingers and spilling it out again like a pirate with a bag of golden coins. "But I'm willing to learn." Suddenly he was smiling again, skimming above the deeper currents. "Are you?"

She wasn't about to answer that. "Why don't we tell crime stories?" she asked brightly instead. "Why don't you tell me all about your biggest cases?"

He laughed, letting his hand curl around to hold the back of her head. "And all about how I got into this profession so you can figure out what's 'wrong' with me? No, thanks, lady shrink. I can do without a session on the couch."

"Suspicious type, aren't you?" she muttered, closing her eyes again. "I think I really should go to my room and get some sleep."

"And you call me suspicious?"

She felt his hand on the back of her neck, rubbing softly, easing her tight muscles. The feeling was so delightfully soothing, she didn't want to stop him.

"You're going to have to stay here, my beautiful captive. I'm not going to let you go."

Beautiful. Funny—she didn't think she'd ever been called that before. Her mother had been beautiful, and a lot of good it had done her in the long run. So Shelley had decided at an early age that she would never count on her own looks, which were fine, but unspectacular. She would count on her brain. And that was exactly what she'd done.

She'd never done anything to draw attention to her looks, and over the years she'd forgotten to look at herself in mirrors. Suddenly she wondered what she looked like, what she really looked like. Could she possibly be beautiful, lying here in agony on a hotel room carpet? Not a chance. Michael really did live in a dreamworld. Either that, or he spoke with a very forked tongue.

"Why don't we get you into bed?" he said softly, very close to her ear. "I'll carry you. . . ."

"No!" She shook her head vigorously. "No, I'm fine right here." She'd seen the bed, all turned back and inviting. And she'd been chilled to the bone.

His strong hand was making magic circles of warmth all across the width of her upper back. "I have no designs on your virtue, Shelley," he told her, his voice edged with irony. "Believe me, I like my women healthy and willing."

Of course, he did, Shelley told herself. And how many of them had there been over the years? She didn't want to think about that. A man with his looks and masculine magnetism—she had no doubt he was seldom without female companionship when he wanted it. The question was, What did he want with her?

"I don't know why you want me to stay," she murmured, stretching under the tantalizing touch of his hand. "I'm not exactly good company this way."

His hand stopped, fingers tightening slightly. "You have a pretty low opinion of the male gender if you think I can't enjoy you without sex," he said shortly, his voice unusually harsh. "I can get sex anywhere." His tone softened. "But a Shelley Pride only comes around once in a million years."

She opened her eyes and looked into his deep, velvet gaze. This wasn't just a line, she decided, a sense of awe growing into wary uncertainty. He really meant it. What could that mean?

Did it mean she could relax and enjoy him too? Did it mean she could let down the barriers and . . . fall in love?

Falling in love. She closed her eyes again as he

continued to massage her. Why did they call it that? It made love sound like a deep hole, a sort of psychic well, that one fell into if one wasn't careful. And then there was the long, long climb back out. Was she ready to take the risk?

"Why did Shelley Pride come around, anyway?" he asked curiously. "How did you happen to fall into my lap twice in a lifetime?"

"Oh—" She avoided his gaze. "Carrie, my room-mate, and I just came down for a few days of vacation."

"What luck." He grinned and she couldn't tell if he was suspicious. "What room are the two of you staying in?"

She told him. "We've only got it for two more nights. Then it's back to work." She yawned and snuggled down into the carpet again, feeling mar-velously relaxed.

She heard the zipper at the back of her dress being lowered and she stirred, ready to protest, but he stopped her with a soft kiss just below her ear. "Don't worry," he whispered. "No ulterior motives. Just relax. Take a nap. Pretend I'm your nanny putting you to bed."

"Nanny Michael." She chuckled at the concept. "Tell me a story, Nanny."

"All I know are ghost stories." He unclasped the back of her strapless bra, giving him free access to her back, from the top of her spine almost to the tip of her tailbone. She scrunched her elbows in, making sure the clothing didn't fall all the way free. For some strange reason she believed him, believed that he wasn't trying to arouse her with his touch. That helped her to relax, and with relaxation came contentment.

"Then tell me a ghost story," she said, and then she yawned sleepily. "A nice scary ghost story to keep me awake."

She could hear the grin in his voice. "How about

a nice boring ghost story to put you to sleep? That's the only kind I know." He shifted his weight so that he could put more grip on the rubbing. Her muscles felt deliciously lazy now, completely limp. "I make this one up as I go along for my eight-year-old niece. It knocks her out in about forty-five seconds. Let's see how long it takes with you."

Shelley lay very still as he began his story. A few hours ago, if he'd told her he sometimes spent time making up bedtime stories for a little girl, she would have thought he was joking. Now she knew better. What other surprises did this man's handsome face mask?

His rambling story concerned a girl named Ginger and a big old-fashioned house with lots of mysterious rooms and things that went *drip-drip-drip* in the night and doors that slammed shut behind her. Shelley didn't really listen to it all. She drifted in and out of the story, in and out of her thoughts, and then closer and closer to sleep.

Michael's hand worked its way across every inch of her back. It was amazing how good that felt, and how close it could come to sensuality without quite going over the edge. Another time, she knew, another place, and a touch like that might send her beyond rationality in seconds. But right now, it merely comforted, though it didn't try to hide the promise of things to come.

Sleepily she wondered what on earth she was doing here, lying on the floor of Michael's hotel room. It was ridiculous really. She should pull herself up and get back to her own room. She knew he would let her go if she made it clear that she really wanted to.

But did she really want to? That was the point, wasn't it?

His voice was as soothing as his hand; low and rumbling, caressing her. She opened her eyes into tiny slits, watching him. As she watched he bent over her, dropping a soft kiss in the small of her back, and suddenly the embers that had been so docile leaped into flame, flaring through the danger zone, and she gasped, pulling up, remembering just in time to hold her dress against her chest.

"Sorry." He grinned sheepishly. "All in all, you've got to admit, I've been pretty good. Haven't I?"

Leaning on one elbow, just as he was, she smiled back at him helplessly, feeling a rush of crazy affection that was even stronger than the desire that had burned in her only seconds before. Every instinct in her body said, "Grab him, take him in your arms, hold on tightly, forget tomorrow," and it took all her strength to stop from doing just that.

"So-so," she said instead, hoping he couldn't tell why her voice was just a little shaky. "But like the man said, it's not over till it's over."

He shrugged, palms up. "I don't know why you're not sound asleep. With my niece it takes no time at all."

She couldn't hold back a grin. "With your niece I doubt if you add the complimentary back rub."

He snapped his fingers. "So that's it."

"Could be."

"How are you feeling?"

"Better." She started to pull herself into a sitting position, still clutching her dress tightly to her. "I'm sure I can walk now. And I really should get back to my room. . . ."

"Not a chance."

She gazed at him, wide-eyed, as he raised to one knee, scooped her up with one arm under her legs and another at her back, and stood with her in his arms.

"It's bedtime for lady shrinks," he told her cheerfully.

"Michael!"

"Hush." In three wide strides he had her lying

back against the fluffy pillows. "Just listen to your nanny, now." He grinned down at her, then went serious. "Shelley, listen to me. I'm not going to try to seduce you tonight. I promise. You're going to sleep in this bed and I'll sleep somewhere else." He gestured toward the chairs. "But tomorrow morning anything goes. Okay?"

She was helpless, utterly helpless. All he had to do was flash those pearly white teeth at her, and she was ready to do whatever he wanted. She let out a long, despairing sigh. "What am I going to sleep in?" she asked hopelessly.

He blinked. "I'll tuck the covers over you if you're shy, and you can pull off your clothes underneath."

"You expect me to sleep in the nude?"

"Why not? I do."

She opened her mouth, but there didn't seem to be any logical way to answer that.

Still, he seemed to understand. "I'm afraid I don't carry spare nighties in my suitcase," he apologized sadly. "I may take it up though. Especially if you promise to keep meeting me like this."

Before she could answer that, he had another idea. "Tell you what. I'll give you one of my T-shirts."

"Your T-shirts?" She still clutched her clothes suspiciously, and started pulling the covers up over them too.

"Sure." He reached into his case and pulled out a large white jersey shirt with short sleeves. "This will fit you as well as any pajama top."

She put out a hand to take it from him, but suddenly he drew it back out of her reach. "Let me," he said softly, his eyes dark and shadowed.

She hesitated, then began to take off her clothes under the covers. There wasn't much to it. He'd already unzipped the dress and unclasped the bra. She had only to wriggle out of them and pull them out from under the covers.

The sheets felt cool and clean against her naked body. "I'm ready," she said, holding her hands out to him. He came toward her slowly, putting the shirt over her head, putting the armholes in position, like a mother dressing a child. But there the similarity ended.

Holding her dark gaze with his brilliant blue one, he slowly shoved back the covers. She didn't stop him. She knew as surely as she knew her name that she couldn't stop him, no matter what he meant to do.

He glanced down at her uncovered breasts. She heard him mutter something under his breath, but she couldn't make out what it was. Then he leaned down and gently kissed first one rosy nipple, then the other, bringing each of them taut and dark in the lamplight before beginning the slow, exquisitely slow, task of drawing the shirt down over them. Shelley held her breath, closing her eyes, not sure if she was trying to avoid facing this moment or trying to extend it as long as possible.

His warm hands slid over her skin, and just before he'd covered her navel, he bent to kiss it. Then he abruptly rose from the bed and started across the room.

"Where are you going?" Darn. He'd think she wanted him to come back and finish what he'd started. And if the truth were known, maybe she did.

"You go to sleep, lady shrink. I've got things to do." He swore softly, shaking his head. "Shelley, I am going into this bathroom to take a cold shower. A very cold shower." He opened the bathroom door, then looked back at her. "In fact, if you should hear a scream, a sort of wolflike cry of despair, coming from this general direction, call room service for ice cubes." And he disappeared into the little room.

Shelley stared at the door as it closed behind him. She heard the sound of the shower and knew that all she had to do was jump up and throw on her dress, then dash out the door, and this whole silly adventure would be over. Didn't he know that?

Of course, he did. He was either too confident in his own powers of attraction to think she'd try to escape—or too trusting. Which was it?

Whatever. She snuggled down into the pillows and yawned. She was going to wait right here and talk to him about it when he came out again.

Six

Shelley woke to find sunlight streaming across the bed in golden shafts of warmth. She raised her head, blinking blearily, and saw Michael at the window, securing the drapes.

For one long second shock froze her. What was she doing here—in a man's room, in a man's bed? Then the events of the previous evening came flooding back, and she relaxed. But only a little.

"So you wake to sunlight, do you?" He'd turned and was watching her. "That's good to know. The alarm didn't do the trick. Neither did the ringing of the phone. And I've spent the last half hour walking heavy and clearing my throat a lot." He grinned. "I even tried singing 'Oh, What a Beautiful Mornin'.' You're lucky you missed that."

She smiled sleepily, then felt for her hair, wondering what she looked like. Probably a raving banshee, she thought with chagrin. Makeup smeared, hair standing on end—how can I slink away without him getting a good look at this mess?

"You look gorgeous." So he was a mind reader. She'd thought as much.

"You look pretty good yourself." Was that really her voice saying that? But it was true. She watched as he walked toward the bed. He was barefoot and barechested, wearing only dark slacks that fit low on his slim hips. The sunlight sprayed around his form like spears, as though he were some kind of golden god. When he sank into the bed and leaned toward her, she smiled, reaching out with one tentative hand to barely touch the tangled hair that matted on his chest, watching her fingers play with the curls, not daring to look into his eyes.

His shoulders looked much broader naked than they did when covered by suit cloth. The muscles were thick and rounded, giving him a powerful look that was something of a contrast to the slimly elegant figure he cut in a well-made suit. He looked real, earthy, and very, very sexy.

"How are you doing this morning?" he asked softly, stretching back a bit as though to enjoy the way she was touching his chest.

"I feel . . ." She hesitated, still not ready to look at him. "I feel fine physically, but kind of out of place socially." She risked a quick glance into his eyes. "Do you know what I mean?"

"Don't worry about that." He moved closer, blotting out the sun. "I'm going to make you feel at home."

He kissed her very softly, barely touching her lips with his own, then again, gently nibbling on her lower lip, moving surely, insistently, against her. She closed her eyes and leaned into her pillows, letting her breasts press into his chest, thrilling slightly to his conquest.

A conquest accomplished without firing a single

shot. She wasn't thinking very clearly yet, but then she didn't really want to think. Much nicer just to feel. Much, much, nicer.

He traced the outline of her lips with his warm tongue. She raised her arms and encircled his neck, pulling all his weight down on top of her, wanting to feel him everywhere, all around her.

"I've been waiting for this all morning," he breathed into her ear. "I thought you'd never wake up."

"Why didn't you wake me?" she whispered back.

"I tried." He raised his head and smiled down at her. "Another few minutes and I would have seduced you while you were sleeping."

She writhed beneath him, every nerve end tingling with sensuous arousal. He wanted her. She wanted him. What could be simpler? She'd never known a man she liked more. Loved more? No, she didn't want to admit to that. That brought with it all sorts of awkward baggage she didn't feel up to opening. Things like tomorrow.

But what did tomorrow matter? Shelley asked herself. They had this moment. Maybe they could stretch it out for a very long time. If they played their cards right.

"Wait!" Suddenly memories resurfaced. "What about the Weekses? Wasn't Margery going to come calling for me at five-thirty, or some nasty time like that? Surely it's way past that now."

He swept the hair back from her eyes and smiled. "She came. I let her see how peacefully you were sleeping, told her I'd convinced you to stay over another day, and she left, happy as a clam."

Shelley giggled. "I can just imagine what you led her to believe. She probably thinks you're some persuasive guy."

He shrugged modestly. "I am."

"Are you?"

"That's just what I'm about to prove to you." He

dropped a kiss on her nose. "If you'll shut up and let me."

She wanted to do just that, and she closed her eyes, reaching for him again. Her hands slipped up into his hair and she opened her eyes in surprise. "Why is your hair so wet?"

"I just took a shower."

She made a face. "Another shower? How many showers do you take?"

"Last night was strictly therapeutic. This morning was more functional."

"Such a clean man," she murmured.

"Such a hungry man," he growled against her ear. His kiss was full of wild, tempting excitement, an intoxicating brew that went straight to her head, leaving her reeling, but reaching for more. His hard male warmth flooded her, and when she felt the covers slip away, she made no move to stop them.

His hand covered her breast, still cloaked by the thin jersey of his T-shirt. "You're so soft," he whispered. "You practically melt away under my hand." His fingers curled around her nipple, already hard and high with excitement. "It's a good thing I've got something to hold on to," he teased.

His touch was exquisite, electric, impossible. Every time his fingers moved, they sent sparks into her bloodstream. When he touched her breasts, the sparks burst into fire, and she moaned out his name, wanting him as she'd never wanted a man before.

His hand went to the hem of the T-shirt and began to pull it up. She felt the heat of his unhindered touch on her stomach, and then his fingers were slipping beneath the elastic of the black nylon panties that were still clinging to her hips, and she gasped as the world seemed to fall away, leaving her floating in space with only his body to cling to.

The T-shirt was gone, the panties were gone, even his slacks had disappeared. His kisses were wild with an urgency that flattered her, making her feel like an impossibly desirable woman, a goddess to equal the god he seemed to her. His passion kindled a like response, and she met his ardor with a hunger of her own.

Suddenly the shrill cry of the telephone split the air with savage insistence. Michael didn't seem to hear it. His hands were stroking her, his lips were testing the most sensitive spot behind her ear, and his body was ready, so ready, to complete what they'd begun.

But Shelley heard the phone. With each ring it bothered her more and more. "Michael, it might be the Weekses," she whispered at last.

He groaned into her hair. "Why can't you ever get a busy signal when you need one?"

Jackknifing away from her, he reached for the receiver, snarled into it, "Not now, call later," jammed it back down on the telephone, thrust the whole contraption under the bed, and was back with her in less time than it took to tell it.

Shelley couldn't help but laugh, but the laughter died in her throat as she was quickly caught up in the vortex of their lovemaking once again. And when he came to her, so clean, so crisp and eager, and when she opened to him, warm and loving and trembling with excitement, they were beyond laughter, beyond tears, sailing in a special heaven reserved for lovers, caught on the cusp of a rainbow, riding the crest of a whirlwind.

And when the wind died away, they lay tangled in a sweet knot, both breathing very hard, still enjoying the feel of each other's bodies.

"Let's do it again," was the first thing Michael said once he'd caught his breath.

"What?"

She rolled aside enough so that she could look into his face.

"Let's do it again," he repeated, reaching for her. "We were interrupted. It wasn't perfect."

She laughed, evading the hand that fumbled for her breast. "It was perfect for me," she protested. "It was wonderful."

He went very still, his blue eyes infinite and sure. "Was it really?" he said, so softly that she realized with sudden astonishment that he really cared whether it was or not. "I want it to be perfect for you. Every time."

She wanted to say *So do I want it to be perfect for you,* but how could she? Instead, she smiled uncertainly and touched his lips with her finger. "It was wonderful," she repeated, suddenly shy.

"It'll get even better." Now he was his cocky self again. "Just wait. The more we practice, the better we'll get."

She looked at him searchingly. He was kidding, of course. This was the man who'd informed her airily that for him relationships didn't even exist. Talk is cheap, Mr. Harper, she said to herself.

"Hand me the T-shirt, please," she asked aloud. "I'm going to need a shower myself now."

"Can't you walk around naked in front of me?" he asked as though merely curious about a sense of modesty he didn't share.

"No," she told him firmly.

"Why on earth not?" He laughed at her, leaning back, his blue eyes shimmering in the sunlight.

"I don't know you well enough yet," she said primly. She used a teasing tone, but she was serious, nonetheless, and he could tell.

He handed her the shirt but shook his head, puzzled. "You know me well enough to sleep in my bed. You know me well enough to make delicious love to me." He ruffled her hair as her head came through the hole at the top of the shirt. "But you don't know me well enough to be unashamed of your nakedness."

"It has nothing to do with shame." Didn't he understand what a giant step she'd taken here? Couldn't he see that this was unusual for her? That she didn't sleep with every man she dated? Good grief, Shelley told herself, she didn't even sleep with men she was attracted to, Of course, there'd been few of them lately. But even nice men, fun men, attractive men, had been locked away from this kind of intimacy with her.

That brought her back to her major problem. Why this man? Why Michael Harper—undercover operator, con man extraordinaire, playboy, drifter? Why had she felt it was so right to sleep with him?

So right, in fact, that she couldn't even regret it now.

What would happen next? She had no idea. He liked her. She could tell that much. But did he really want her around any longer, now that— But she wouldn't think about that.

She jumped up from the bed, needing movement to still her restlessness. "All things in their proper place, at their proper time." She spied the breakfast trays on the table in the corner. "Ooooh, I'm starved! What's to eat?" she said, and started for the food.

"Oh, well." Michael sighed, giving up on the nudity. "I've got to admit, you do look cute in my T-shirt. You poke out in such great places."

Everything he did and said made her want to smile. She glanced down at herself. "You would like that, I suppose," she answered lightly. "It doesn't do a whole lot for me."

"Think we could get it to stay that way?" he asked, casually rising from the bed and coming along behind her. He was oblivious to his own nakedness, perfectly at home with it.

"What do you mean?" she asked, pausing before pouring herself a cup of coffee from the vacuum pot.

"Maybe I could get it bronzed," he mused, cocking his head and looking at the shirt and how it fit her.

"Not with me in it!" she cried.

He came closer, talking low, reaching for her. "But how else are we going to get it to stick out here . . . and here . . . and all these yummy round places down here. . . ."

The coffee was forgotten, and she was in his arms again, his large hands gripping her bottom, his face nuzzling into her neck.

"Michael," she choked out, "you take my breath away. Do you know that?"

"Sure." He nipped at her neck. "It's all part of my unnerving charm." And he gave her earlobe a little kiss.

Just as long as it's not all part of an act as well, Shelley thought. She bit her lip. Now where had that ugly thought come from? Shaken, she pulled out of Michael's embrace.

"What do you want with a bronzed T-shirt anyway?" she asked quickly, pouring out her cofee with a trembling hand.

"Not just any bronzed T-shirt." He flopped down in one of the chairs and picked at a cold breakfast roll that was sitting on a porcelain dish on the tray. "One that exactly duplicates your lovely form."

She slipped into a chair facing him. "Need a new planter, do you?" she quipped, avoiding his eyes. "Just don't pot me with marigolds. They make me sneeze."

"Planter!" He threw down the sweet roll in disgust. "I don't want a planter. I want a reminder of you. And of the miracles you can accomplish in filling out my clothes."

A reminder? A souvenir? What's wrong with the

real thing, Mr. Harper? Has it ever occurred to you that making a commitment, establishing a relationship, could have its own rewards?

No, she didn't suppose it had. He was the man who couldn't afford to get too close to anyone. He'd told her that from the first. It wasn't like he was asking her for anything under false pretenses. She'd known the rules before she entered the game. So why did the coffee taste so bitter in her throat?

The telephone rang, sounding muffled and slightly offended from underneath the bed.

"You see?" Michael said brightly as he dove for it. "They always call back."

He brought the phone to the table, talking as he came. She thought at first it must be the Weekses on the line, but when he gave her a delighted wink, as though he'd made some sort of coup, she realized it must be someone else.

"Absolutely," he was saying. "We'll be there in an hour."

She mouthed *Who?* and he snatched up a pencil and wrote *Mr. Big* on a handy napkin.

"Sorry about hanging up on you before," he was saying into the receiver. "But you know how it is. My little wife came for a surprise visit last night, and . . . well, we hadn't quite finished saying howdy, if you know what I mean."

Shelley groaned and covered her face with her hands while Michael grinned at her wickedly.

"Sure thing. I'm just as anxious to see the property as you are to show it, believe me. And now that my wife is here, we'll be able to make a decision on the spot. Right. Right. See you soon."

The receiver hit the cradle with a crash, and Michael let out a whoop that nearly split Shelley's eardrums. "Hook, line, and sinker!" He slapped the palm she stretched out in question like an athlete after a slam dunk. "We did it, Shelley! We got him."

"Got whom? What are you talking about?" But she was laughing right back at him. He did that to her every time. His good spirits were contagious. "Who is this Mr. Big?" She shook her head. "Mr. Big. Honestly. More shades of Jimmy Cagney movies."

He ignored her digs. "We got through to the top man in the organization. The Weekses are fronts, of course. They lure in the suckers. When they really feel secure, and think the plum is ripe for the picking, they call in the biggie." He grinned at her. "Your arrival from Tulsa must have really added the touch of reality I needed. When Margery saw you sleeping like a baby this morning, she was convinced. She must have called Stickler right away."

"And he called you."

"Right. He'll meet us at the site at eleven."

"Us?"

She could see by the look on his face that he had no doubt about her going along with this wild ride. "Of course, us. We make great partners, don't you think?" His smile might have seduced her on the spot if her mind hadn't been preoccupied. "He's expecting to see Mr. and Mrs. Daniels, and that's whom he'll see."

"Explain to me just what these people are trying to do."

"Cheat me out of all my money." He leaned back and looked at her. "They set up meetings at condominiums, posing as the owners. Or sometimes they really do own them. Then they take on buyers. When they've made enough money, they skip town and the poor buyers find out they've bought property that wasn't up for sale, or, as I think we'll find out in this case, they've paid for the same property five or six other people have paid for, and nobody has a valid deed. A lot of people lose their shirts, the money they were counting on for retirement."

He raised an eyebrow. "Wouldn't you like to put away crooks like that?"

Of course, she'd do it. She couldn't seriously contemplate a way out of it. She'd probably go out on the balcony and sing "Oh, What a Beautiful Mornin' " to the multitudes if he asked her to. But she needed a little time alone, time to think.

"I'd better hurry up and take my shower, then." She stood up. "Oh, my gosh! What am I going to do for clothes? I can't wear your T-shirt to meet Mr. Big."

"No problem." He pointed out her suitcase, sitting on the case rack. "I called your roommate last night, after you went to sleep. She let me in to get your suitcase."

She didn't know whether to be impressed by his helpfulness or incensed by Carrie's lack of suspicion. "She did that? For all she knew, you could have been an ax murderer holding me hostage!"

"Are you kidding?" He threw her a scornful glance before sipping the last of his coffee. "Some women don't have to be convinced about me, you know. Some of them just know instinctively what sort of guy I am."

"That's exactly what I mean." She grinned at him. "And she gave you her blessings anyway. What a friend! But remind me to give her a call and tell her my plans for the day." She started into the bathroom.

"Hold on," he called after her. "I'm coming too."

For once she put her foot down. "No, you aren't." She closed the door until only a crack let her finish talking to him. "This is one mission I plan to go on alone."

"It's a nice big bathtub," he said, his eyes large and a bit woebegone.

"You've already had two showers in the last twelve hours," she protested. "Besides, I need some time alone."

"Oh, no." He groaned. "Don't tell me you need time to think over our relationship."

"Well, what if I do?"

"Just don't think all the fun right out of it," he grumbled, but he'd obviously given up on changing her mind. "And hurry up. It's boring out here without you."

She expected to feel a sense of relief when she'd shut him out, but somehow it didn't come. "It's boring in here without you too," she whispered, then shook her head. It was hopeless. She was crazy about him, and she knew it.

She stood under the stinging spray of the shower and tried to work out what she was doing, where she was going, but facts and feelings floated around her, solutions just out of reach, and she began to wonder if she'd lost all ability to reason.

She'd just made love, the most glorious love of her life, with a man she'd met first as a thief, then as a con man. He was doing both for legal reasons, but that didn't change the fact that he made his living, lived his life, based on fantasy. What part could she play in a dreamworld?

No part at all. Hadn't he made that clear from the start? You're the psychologist, Shelley. You figure it out.

She patted herself dry with the huge white towel, then wrapped it around her body, tucking in the ends, and stepped out into the room.

Michael had dressed. He wore the dark slacks and had put on a crisp white shirt. The cuffs and collar were still unbuttoned, and she stopped a moment, holding her breath, marveling at how handsome he looked, his dark hair and tanned skin set off by the snowy whiteness of his shirt.

He turned at the same moment, but he didn't say a word. The usual glint of humor was missing from his eyes as he stared back at her. The tension stretched between them. Shelley wasn't thinking in words, she was only feeling, and he seemed to be doing exactly the same.

Don't fall in love, Shelley Pride. Don't be such a fool as to fall in love with this wonderful man. The warning blazed through her, but she knew it was too late.

He was moving toward her, and she had a sudden impulse to see what would happen if she met him halfway. Would he pull away her towel and hold her, heedless of his fresh clothes? Could she make him forget all about the appointment with Mr. Big? Tempting, very tempting to find out. But not her style somehow.

"Did you miss me?" she said quickly, turning and pulling open her suitcase before he could reach her. "What should I wear to meet this crime kingpin you're taking me to?"

His hand touched the back of her head as she bent over the clothes, fingers spiking through her shower-damp hair. "Just wear a smile," he said softly. "That's all you need for me."

Her breath stopped in her throat. She wanted more than anything else in the world to turn into his hand, into his embrace, but she steeled herself. "That may be all I need for you," she said lightly, rummaging through her things, "but I think Mr. Big would be a little taken aback. Don't you?"

"Maybe." Suddenly he drew his hand away as though he realized what would happen if he didn't and knew he had to resist temptation. Then the humor was back in his voice. "But if he's as smart as I think he is, he'd never let on."

He sat back on the bed and she pulled out a slacks set—white pants and a sailor top—and held them out for him to examine. "Does this look like something Julie Daniels would wear?" she asked.

He nodded. "Looks fine to me." A look of dismay crossed his face as she turned back toward the bathroom. "Hey, aren't you going to let me watch you dress?"

"Of course not." She flashed a wary look his way.

He jumped up from the bed and beat her to the bathroom door. "You know, we're going to have to do something about this body fixation you have," he told her sternly. "It's not healthy. What are you afraid of?"

You, she started to say, but she stopped herself in time. "Not a thing," she answered instead. She wanted to push her way on into the privacy of the bathroom, but as she looked up into his eyes she hesitated. There was something so open about him. She almost felt she could tell him anything. Maybe he deserved more of an explanation.

"I'm not used to this, you know," she told him, a little shy. "I—I don't do this kind of thing. I've never really lived with a man and I—I can't change quite that fast."

His lopsided grin was delightedly disarming. "No problem." His large hand cupped her chin and he beamed into her dark eyes. "We'll take it a step at a time. Like—"

"The sushi." She said it at the same time he did, and they grinned at each other.

"Get in there and change," he growled, patting her bottom, "before I tear that towel off and ravish you again."

She did as she was told, but the glow he conjured in her didn't fade when she left him. Was this love? If it was, it was wonderful.

Seven

"Have you ever met Mr. Big before?" Shelley asked as they drove along the bay, on the way to the condominium Mike Daniels was supposed to be thinking about buying. The early-summer day was perfect, the sky crystal-blue, the sun as yellow as a California lemon, the ocean water slick and shiny. Expensive white yachts making toward the open sea took down their brilliant blue canvas coverings and hoisted rainbow sails. Pink geraniums bloomed from window ledges, yellow roses and red portulaca lined the road. Colors seemed to pop out at her everywhere she looked. Had it always been this beautiful here, or was there something special about the company?

"I think it's time we started referring to him as Mr. Stickler," Michael answered, maneuvering the car skillfully through the heavy traffic. "It wouldn't do to slip up and call him Mr. Big to his face."

"Think that might give him pause, do you?" she asked, holding back a smile.

"Could be. I don't think I'll chance it." He glanced across the car at her. "I hate bucket seats." He sighed. "When I was a teenager, I always had my girl right next to me."

"One hand on the wheel and one arm around your baby, huh?"

"Absolutely. Keep those women under control."

"Dreamer." She sneaked a glance at him. She could see him as a teenager. Had he worn his hair slicked back, black-leather-jacket style, or had he been strictly Ivy League? From what she knew of him, it could have been either. Maybe both. "But you haven't told me about Mr. B—Stickler. What do you know about him?"

"Quite a lot actually. We've got a very thick file on the man at the department." He pulled into a security area and told the guard where they were going before turning back to Shelley. "Stickler is only one of many aliases. He's done time in Florida for real estate scams, and now he's trying his luck here."

They turned down a side road and approached a row of gleaming new condos sitting at the water's edge. "He started his career in New York when he was pretty young, running numbers for the mob. But that action was a little too risky for him. Job security isn't what it once was. Besides, he wanted to strike out on his own. So he split for Miami."

"White-collar crime is more to his liking than the rough and tumble of the street?"

"Exactly." Michael parked behind a shiny Rolls-Royce. "Besides, the perks are so much nicer," he said, nodding toward the beautiful car.

"Is that his?"

"I imagine so. It's the only other car out here."

She looked at it, shaking her head. "Wouldn't you think he might be afraid his pigeons might get a little shaky seeing that car? I mean, it's obvious where he got the money to buy it. He's not exactly involved in charity work here. He had to make it out of the hides of his clients."

Michael grinned. "But you see, pigeons, as you so eloquently call them, don't look at it that way. They see a man like Stickler as a successful businessman. They only want to get in on the action, to become a part of that success too."

"So it's the old story that greed makes you into a victim of these creeps."

"It often works out that way. Of course, a lot of totally innocent people get caught up in it too."

She took a deep breath. "Anything else I should know before we go in?"

"No. Just be yourself." He got out of the car and came around to her side to open the door for her. "They say he likes women," he added as she rose to join him. "Charm him."

"Oh, brother." She gave him a look of disgust and began the walk up the flagstone steps alongside him.

"Oh, one more thing." He stopped her just before the double front door, a hand on her arm, speaking in a low, careful tone. "Whatever you do, don't say a thing about his hairpiece. He's very sensitive about that."

As if she would bring it up casually in conversation! What did he think she was, an idiot? Her mouth opened, but he didn't give her time to speak.

"In fact," he whispered as he jabbed at the bell, "just to be safe, don't mention hair at all."

There was no time to ask any questions. The door was opening, and she steeled herself to play the part of the perfect suburban housewife, while at the same time remembering to avoid looking at the man's toupee.

"Hello, hello, welcome, come right on in. You

must be the Danielses, right? Please, come right in."

Mr. Stickler was a few inches under six feet, a slightly paunchy, olive-skinned man in a light plaid suit, with snapping black eyes, a perpetual smirk, a bushy mustache, and no hairpiece that Shelley could see.

His hair was quite thin on top. In fact, he'd combed a few strands in such a way as to pretend there was more hair there than he could really muster. But that wasn't a hairpiece. Was it?

He didn't look like a crook. But then, who did? She smiled mechanically, acknowledging the introduction and shaking the man's hand, but her gaze kept straying to the top of his head. If that was a hairpiece, they were making them strangely these days.

Don't even mention hair, Michael had said. That seemed a little extreme. Why would she be likely to mention hair anyway?

"Lathe and plaster," Mr. Stickler was saying, marching them through the rooms. "You can see the quality in every inch of the place."

They were nice units. There was a complex of ten of them, grouped around a common courtyard and built so that every one of them had a nice view of the bay, and even of the jetty, looking out to the open sea, from the two best ones. They were newly built and still unfurnished. Two bedrooms with loft. Just right for upper-level corporate executives from Los Angeles who wanted a weekend retreat at the beach. The whole complex was obviously an ideal investment if the money was right.

Mr. Stickler was still selling like crazy. "Look at this workmanship. Look, look here at these built-in shelves. We had real craftsmen working here, not your regular construction crew that someone hires out of the local bar. These men were imported from Europe. Every man was a master in his field."

"No women?" Shelley saw Michael glance at her in surprise, but she didn't care. He wanted a real Julie Daniels, he was going to get one. Why couldn't Julie be a homegrown feminist?

"Women?" Mr. Stickler was looking at her as though she'd asked how many Martians had been represented.

Shelley smiled a bright, Julie Daniels smile. "Yes, Mr. Stickler. Women."

A cloud passed over his face, then his hustler-style charm took over again and he bristled his mustache at her, giving her what he would have called a smile. "Call me Harry, little lady. No need to be formal."

"H-Harry?" Don't even mention hair, Michael had said, and now the man's name turned out to be Harry? For just a second she smelled a rat. She stuttered over the name, glancing sharply at Michael, but his face was all wide-eyed innocence. There was no time to think it through. Maybe he hadn't known the first name the man was using. She'd still avoid saying the word *hair,* and she'd avoid looking for the hairpiece that didn't seem to be there. And in the meantime she'd better push on ahead with the feminist persona she'd started and ignore the rest.

"There are a lot of women in construction these days, H-Harry. And I say, more power to them. After all, who would know better about how to lay out a house than a woman?"

Harry didn't like feminists. That much was clear. He'd lost his smile, and his mouth had taken on almost a sneer. "There's more to a house than the kitchen," he said, obviously still trying hard to be jovial and finding it very difficult.

Shelley wasn't sure why she'd gotten into this discussion, but she'd started it and now she couldn't think of a graceful way out. All she could do was go on with it. "Oh, come on now, you're splitting hairs," she said, then blanched. She hadn't said that. She couldn't have said that. It wasn't a phrase she'd ever used before in her life. She swayed slightly, staring at Mr. Stickler, and there was Michael behind him, waving at her furiously, as though to remind her not to mention hair.

I didn't, she wanted to shout. That wasn't me. But all she could do was gape at Mr. Stickler, wondering about his hairpiece, and finally Michael stepped in and saved the moment.

"You'll have to excuse Julie," he said smoothly, coming alongside her and taking her arm. "She does get on her soapbox when she gets the chance." He hugged her and gave her a nauseatingly condescending kiss on the forehead. "She's so cute when she gets worked up over something." Then he dropped her like a hot potato and turned back to Harry.

"I can see that the place is a beauty. What I want to study now is the paperwork. Give me some facts and figures, man."

He took them into the den, where he had books and files full of charts and graphs and an expensively printed prospectus. He and Michael went over interest rates and rates of return on investment and escrow fees and tax credit potential and all the other details while Shelley tried not to notice how the ceiling lights reflected off the top of the man's head.

Michael was so very good at this. He looked so eager and happy, just like a man who'd found the perfect way to make his fortune. She could hardly hold back a smile as she watched him. She wanted to reach out and touch his face. Everything he did seemed to grab at her heart. If this was love, so far it felt great.

Thinking about Michael, she glanced absently at Harry's head just in time to find his gaze on her, a slight frown showing that he'd noticed her obsession with his dome. She looked away quickly. That man wasn't wearing a hairpiece. He couldn't be.

"Well, Harry," Michael said at last, rising from his chair. "I think you and I have got ourselves a deal here."

"Wonderful." The man fairly oozed satisfaction. "That's just wonderful. All we need to do is meet at my office in town to draw up the final papers and—heh-heh—exchange funds. And you two will be set to see your money go right out and make money for you, just like it was getting itself a job. Heh-heh-heh."

They all laughed at his little joke, and he began to usher them through the house again, heading toward the front door.

"I'll call my bank in Tulsa," Michael was saying. "I've already made arrangements to have my money available at a moment's notice. I can meet you in town by two o'clock."

"Wonderful!" Harry fairly bounced with glee. "You'll find this to be a wonderful investment. People are lining up already to buy into the individual units. They're the best on the bay."

Shelley found the man utterly annoying, and his joy set her teeth on edge. She couldn't resist saying something to deflate him a little.

"I guess people out here don't have much choice, do they? I mean, there are so many people and such limited housing available."

He stiffened and she smiled sunnily. "These places are nice, of course, but hardly perfect. Why, look at this, H-Harry." She was never going to be able to say that name again without stuttering and thinking of hairpieces and con men. She walked over to the window that looked out over the water. "The sun coming in through here is going to ruin this hardwood floor in no time." She scuffed her foot along the polished surface. "You ought to get yourself a little rug and put it down. . . ." Her voice trailed off, and she turned beet-red, looking out of the corner of her eye at where a nice little rug might have added some fur to Harry. She hadn't said that. Oh, please, why couldn't she stay away from the subject?

Now she was thoroughly ashamed of herself as she saw the poor man, looking puzzled, slowly lift his hand and pat the top of his head, wondering, no doubt, just what it was she kept staring at.

She'd been a complete failure at this undercover work, that was for sure. Michael had wanted a nice, suburban housewife and he'd gotten a feminist agitator. He'd warned her not to mention hair and she hadn't been able to stay away from the word. He must be really sorry he'd brought her along. This undercover work was a real strain, and she was incompetent at it.

She couldn't take any more. Mumbling something unintelligible that she meant for good-bye, she whirled out the front door, walking quickly down the path toward the car. But she hadn't taken many steps before she heard clearly what Michael said to the man, even though she was past the bushes that shielded her from sight of the doorway.

"Don't mind her. You know how women are." She could hear the grin in his voice. "Hair today," he said as clear as a bell. "Gone tomorrow."

Shelley stopped in her tracks. She'd only suspected it before, but now she knew she'd been taken. How could Michael have done that to her? "Why you . . . !" She turned on him furiously as he came up behind her.

"Not now," he said through a clenched smile. "Save it up for when we're out of sight."

She wanted to belt him in the jaw, and she'd

never hit another human being in her life. She got into the car next to him and stared straight ahead.

"Let me know when we're out of sight," she said evenly. "I want to know when it's safe to kill you."

"Just hold on to that thought," he teased, "until we're totally out of the complex. I know a place where we can go to talk."

She sat as tight as a coiled spring, furious. He'd set her up from the very beginning. Why on earth had he done that?

Michael drove them quickly through the security post and out onto the highway, then turned the car into a drive-in. "I need a drink. How about you?"

She nodded slowly, lips pressed together. "I think I could use one," she admitted, still holding back her slow simmer.

"Two super-size chocolate malts," Michael told the girl on roller skates who came to the window of the car to take their order. "With a shot of chocolate syrup on the side."

Shelley felt as though she were about to explode. She waited until the girl left the window before she asked the question she'd been waiting to ask for a very long time, speaking with careful, strained precision. "That man didn't have on a hairpiece, did he?"

Michael was forthright in his answer. "No, he didn't."

She let out her breath in a long, angry sigh. "Then why did you tell me he did?"

He shrugged, all innocence. "I thought he might have bought one by now."

"Michael Harper, that is no answer! Why did you do that to me?"

"For fun. Wasn't it fun?"

"Not for me!"

"Well, it was for me. Did you see his face when you told him to get a rug?"

"Michael!" She leaned over as though to shake

some sense into him and he took hold of her shoulders and kissed her, hard and long, until her anger faded and her response to him came seeping back into the forefront of her consciousness.

"Oh, Michael." She snuggled into his arms, sitting on the brake and not caring a bit. "You really shouldn't have done that."

"You're right." His arms tightened around her, and he buried his face in her hair. "Actually I should never have taken you with me at all. It's against department policy to involve civilians in these things. And rightly so." He sighed. "And I wouldn't have taken you if I'd thought there was any chance at all of danger. But I knew all about Harry. He's a slimy little weasel, but he doesn't like rough stuff."

"So why did you take me?" she asked curiously.

He kissed her nose. "Because I didn't want you out of my sight. Now, sit up straight. Here come the malts."

She sat up straight and drank her malt, but something lacking in his explanations still troubled her. "Why did you take the chance of setting me up that way about the hairpiece? What if the whole goofy affair had put Harry off, made him suspicious?"

He grinned at her like a boy in a baseball cap, hiding the ball that had just broken the plate-glass window behind his back. "It was a tame setup. It needed something to liven it up."

"What?" She still wasn't sure she understood.

"It's a habit I've sort of fallen into lately. I do things like that when the going gets too routine. Makes life a little more exciting."

A cold chill was working its way down her spine. "Do you always consider it boring unless you're getting shot at?" she asked.

His grin was as wide as a devil's swath. "Sometimes even then," he admitted. "Come on, drink up. I've got to get to that meeting in town."

She sat very still as they drove back to the hotel. Michael Harper was a wonderful, sexy, thrilling man, Shelley told herself. She was a little bit in love with him. More the fool she. A man like this, a man so hooked on excitement that he even upped the ante when he didn't have to, was never going to settle for a tame psychologist to round out his life. She felt a very empty hole where happiness had warmed her only hours before. It had been a wonderful vacation, but it seemed the holiday was almost over.

"I can't take you with me to the final meet in town," he told her as they left the elevator for his room. "The boys from the department will be there when it goes down, and even a slimy weasel like Harry can get mean when he's cornered."

"You mean, you're going to be arresting him?"

Michael nodded, inserting his key in the door. "We've got enough on this character to put him away for a long time. He didn't own that condo he was trying to sell us, and now I've got proof."

Shelley walked slowly into the room and looked around. The maid had been in, and every bit of evidence of the night they'd had together—and the morning—had been obliterated. The bed was made up and looked square and uninviting. All the clothes were hung carefully in the closet. And the air conditioner was on full blast, chilling the room that had been so warm before.

Maybe that was why she felt cold. But somehow Shelley was afraid it had to do with more than the temperature. She walked to the sliding glass door that opened onto the balcony and stood looking out, arms folded tightly across her chest.

Michael was making calls on the telephone. Shelley didn't pay much attention to them. She knew he was calling his department and coordinating with the police officers who were in on the operation. She watched the sailboats on the bay and tried not to think at all.

That, of course, was impossible. She was a thinking woman, after all. "Relationships don't exist," he'd told her when they'd first met. "I can't afford to get too close to anyone." He'd said his time was too short in any one place. That letting down emotional barriers would make him vulnerable.

She'd thought he needed counseling to confront his rationalizations of an avoidance syndrome. Now she was afraid that she was the one who was going to need help. But she was sure of one thing: This was the last she would see of Michael Harper.

Michael's arms slid around her from behind and he pulled her back against his broad chest. "Let's go sailing tomorrow," he said softly against her hair. "We'll take a picnic lunch and find a deserted beach somewhere. . . ."

Despite her unease she chuckled. "Lots of luck." Then the smile faded. She didn't want to answer his invitation outright, because she didn't want to get involved in an argument at this point. "Do you know how to sail?"

"Of course, I know how to sail. I know how to do almost everything." His boast was so little-boy proud, she had to hold back her laughter. "And if I don't know how, I'll learn."

He turned her, kissing her soundly and then looking down at her, his eyes shining with something—what was it? Affection? Humor? She wasn't sure, but whatever it was, it was irresistible.

"You're pretty cocky, aren't you?" she said teasing him. "You think you're pretty hot stuff."

"I *am* hot stuff," he shot back. "Want me to prove it again?"

"Not right now," she answered. "Memories will have to suffice."

"Only for a little while." His face came down gently against her cheek, rubbing back and forth in a warm, sensual caress. "But it'll seem like forever. Be in bed when I get back. Okay?"

She ignored the implications of that request, looking up at him with surprise. "Are you going to be that late?"

"Yeah." He grinned. "It might be as late as four o'clock this afternoon."

"Michael!" She laughed, caught again in the magic of his warmth.

"Can I help it if I want to make love to you again?" He kissed her neck. "And again and again. . . ."

She sighed, closing her eyes. His touch was a bright piece of heaven.

"What are you going to do while I'm gone?"

Her silence had made him suspicious, she decided. But it was best not to come right out with the truth. He'd fight it. She wasn't up to that.

If she were brave and strong, she would tell him the truth right now. He deserved as much. But she wasn't strong, she was finding out. She wasn't strong and she might give in to his arguments. Much safer not to let him make them.

"I'm not sure," she told him. "I might write a letter." That much was true. He didn't have to be told the letter was to him.

"Good." He let her go. "Just as long as you're here when I get back."

Luckily that wasn't a question and she didn't have to answer it. Instead, on impulse, she went up on tiptoe and kissed his lips. "You're a very special person, Michael," she said, her voice husky. "I'm glad we ran into each other last night."

And she was too. Whatever painful residue she would carry away from this encounter, it had been well worth it. She would never forget him, or the time they'd spent together.

He looked a little surprised, but he didn't seem to sense the despair behind her words. "I'm glad too," he said, stroking her hair. "You saved me the trouble of coming looking for you."

"Looking for me?" She made a skeptical face. "Are you trying to tell me that was in your plans?" And yet why not? It had certainly been in hers. She'd gone looking for him, looking for trouble. What insanity had ruled her? Hadn't she realized how impossible it would be to fall in love with him? He'd warned her, after all. And still, she hadn't been able to stay away.

"Absolutely." Something wavered in his bright blue eyes. "Well, not exactly," he admitted reluctantly.

She didn't know whether to be hurt by the admission or flattered that he didn't seem to be able to lie to her. "Somehow I had a feeling it might not have been."

His face took on an earnest expression that erased all the lines of humor. "You made a big impression on me, Shelley, right from the first. And when you responded with all that delicious fire in your office . . . well, when I left you there, I had no intention of trying to see you again. I've told you before relationships don't mesh with this job." He shook his head, his eyes dark. "But I kept thinking about you all week."

He sounded surprised, as though he wasn't used to remembering women that way. She wanted to glow with the pleasure his words aroused, but she couldn't. She wished he hadn't started this exercise in candor. It wasn't going to make it any easier to do what had to be done. Somehow she had to turn this around and get them back on a light, breezy plane. If he said much more along these lines, she'd end up sobbing in his arms. Just to imagine him thinking about her all week . . . "Well, they do say it's the thought that counts, don't they?"

It didn't take much to tickle his funny bone. The grin was quickly back. "It was more than a thought, really," he said, tongue firmly in cheek. "You stuck in my mind like a sticky burr, prickly and annoying. You know what I mean? Like an itch I couldn't reach."

"An itch, huh?" She cocked her head to the side, eyes bright and sassy. "What happens now that you've scratched it?"

His eyes blazed, and she jumped away, sensing the attack of a tickler, but he grabbed hold of her before she could escape, tilting her back until they both collapsed, laughing, onto the bed. "It turns out to be a serious rash. A terminal disease," he growled, holding her down. "I'm going to need constant therapy."

His hand slid in under her blouse, cupping her breast, and his mouth took possession of hers, lighting a fire with his tongue, his body moving against her with a growing urgency that started a twisting, writhing sensation in the pit of her stomach.

"This is therapy?" she gasped when he finally let her up for air.

"The very best." He shook his head ruefully. "But I've only got time for a limited dose right now." He shifted his weight, freeing her. "Duty calls."

He touched her cheek with his index finger, slowly tracing a pattern while he watched, bemused, then he gathered himself and rose from the bed. Turning away, he stripped off his sport coat and opened his suitcase. She sat up and watched, eyes wide, as he took out a revolver in a holster and strapped it to his shoulder, then put the sport coat back on again.

"Do you think you're going to need that?" she asked, her voice shaky.

"You never know. I've had to use it on occasion." Then he saw her face and he stepped over to draw her up into his arms again. "Hey, no big deal. Believe me, I've been in this business for a long time and I've never been badly hurt yet."

"Just a little hurt?" she asked in a quavery squeak.

He made a face. "Just a very little. A scratch. A skinned nose. Nothing worse. Really."

"You swear it?"

He held his hand up in a Boy Scout salute. "I swear it," he said solemnly. "And I'd never lie to you."

The gun panicked her. She didn't want him hurt. The thought of someone hurting him made her feel very fierce, as though she would hunt down anyone who did anything to him and break them with her bare hands. And even that reaction stunned her. She'd never felt so strongly protective of anyone before. A whole new aspect of her personality to explore.

"Maybe I should come along . . ."

"No." He was coming on very domineering all of a sudden. "You can't. You wait here." He let her go, and the look in his eyes told her his mind was already on the job ahead. "See you soon." And he was out the door.

Just like that. "Good-bye, Michael," she whispered into the empty room. "It's been nice." She felt hollow, like a child the day after Christmas. It was over.

Waiting to give him time to leave the hotel, she let herself out of the room and took the elevator to the floor where Carrie and she had booked their room.

"Well, there you are." Carrie greeted her with a wide grin. She was sitting in the middle of one of the twin beds, applying scarlet polish to the tips of her toes. Her short chestnut-brown hair shone silkily as she talked, bouncing when she nodded her head to emphasize points.

She carefully set aside her bottle of nail polish. "Listen, I met your hunk last night. If that's the kind of man you psychologists get to work on in your clinic, I'm heading back to college for my degree. Wow!"

"Carrie, I'm sorry about deserting you last night. It was really a strange thing, I don't know—"

"Are you kidding?" Carrie bounced up and down on the bed like a teenage girl who'd just heard her favorite rock star was in the lobby. "It was fantastic! It was the most romantic thing I ever saw! The way he swept you off your feet . . ." She swooned dramatically across the bed, then grinned. "When's the wedding?"

Shelley kicked off her shoes and flopped down on the bed beside her, lying on her stomach and resting her head on her folded arms. "There's not going to be any wedding, Carrie. It's not like that at all."

"Give it time." Her friend nodded wisely. "He's crazy about you. I could tell. When he came to get your suitcase, he kept asking questions . . ."

Shelley raised her head. "What questions?"

". . . and telling me cute little things about you . . ."

"What did you tell him?"

". . . and saying things like 'I hope you don't mind if I monopolize your friend for a while. Like maybe the rest of her life.' "

"He didn't say anything of the sort!"

Carrie sighed. "Well, he would've if he'd thought of it."

And that shows how accurate your intuition is, Carrie my friend, Shelley thought sadly. "What questions?" she repeated aloud.

Carrie's smile was smug. "You wouldn't want me to betray a confidence, would you?"

Shelley glared at her, rising as though ready to back up her threat. "You wouldn't want me to throw all your underclothes off the balcony, would you?"

"Watch out for the toes!" Carrie wriggled her still-drying toenails at Shelley. The pout on her pretty red mouth looked almost real. "Boy, give the girl a lover, and she turns on her best friend," she complained.

"Carrie!"

"Okay, okay." She sat up, cross-legged, and obviously relishing her role. "He wanted to know what you liked for breakfast—"

"And you told him nothing but black coffee."

"Right. Then he asked if there was some man lurking around in your life, someone he was going to have to outfight or outsmart in order to win you."

"He didn't say that! "

"He most certainly did. He didn't put it quite that way, but that was the gist of it." Carrie gasped. "My God, you're blushing!"

Shelley flopped back down on her stomach, hiding her face. "I am not," she replied, her voice muffled. But she knew she was. Oh, Michael, Michael, why did you have to be so lovable?

"It's finally happened." Carrie was so entranced by her friend's romance, she forgot to tease. "You're in love, aren't you? Really head-over-heels in love."

Shelley peered out from under her arm. "I've been in love before," she said grumpily. "Don't act like it's the end of the world."

Carrie shook her head firmly. "If you mean that schoolgirl fling with Barry, forget it. You never really loved the man. When you found out he had another girl stashed away, you were so relieved, you ended up being her best friend."

That was a novel way of looking at her heartbreak. But Shelley had to admit Carrie had a point. The romance with Barry hadn't come close to touching her as deeply as Michael did. And she barely knew him! What might it be like to really get to know him, to spend her life— Forget it. There was no chance, and thinking about it would only bring more pain.

"This is different," Carrie went on. "The man is different. I knew the moment I saw you two together that you were made for each other. You looked so perfect sitting at that table down at the Boar's Head. As though you were already man and wife."

Shelley couldn't resist a smile. Little did Carrie know!

"He told me his name was Michael. But that's about all I know about him, except that he's gorgeous. Where does he live? What does he do for a living?"

What indeed. Shelley hesitated, not sure what she was allowed to tell. Of course, she trusted Carrie implicitly, but it wasn't her secret. She couldn't do anything that might possibly put Michael in jeopardy. He lived a shadow life, a life she couldn't share. She sighed, avoiding Carrie's eyes. "It doesn't matter. I'm not going to see him again."

For once Carrie was so flabbergasted, she couldn't think of a thing to say. She sat staring at Shelley, her mouth hanging open.

"I know we've got reservations for another night," Shelley went on, sitting up on the bed, "but I've got to get out of here. You stay, if you want, and I'll take a cab home."

"You just hold on a minute." Carrie had her stubborn face on. "I'm not going to let you do this."

Shelley glanced at her friend, then away. "Oh, Carrie, you don't know. . . ."

Carrie grabbed her hand and squeezed it. "I know, all right. I know you. You've fallen hard and you're scared to death, so you want to run back and hide in your books and cases, where it's nice and safe and boring."

"No." She shook her head sadly. "That's not it. You don't know the background of all this."

Carrie bounced on the bed in her impatience. "I don't have to know the background to recognize a woman running from love when I see one. And you're the one who's supposed to know all about what makes people tick!" She took Shelley's shoulders in her hands to make her meet her eyes. "Physician, heal thyself!"

"Oh, Carrie!" Shelley broke away from her grip and rose from the bed, pacing the floor with restless unhappiness. "Someday I'll be able to tell you all about it, and then you'll see how wrong you are. I've got to go."

Carrie frowned. "I don't think he'll let you." she said flatly.

Shelley stopped in front of the mirror. Oh, what can ail you, sad, sad lady, she thought to herself in a paraphrase of the Keats poem. That's what she looked like. Alone and palely loitering. A vagabond on a darkling plain. "He's not here," she said softly, and her voice sounded far away. "He left for a business appointment. I'm going to be gone by the time he comes back."

"Oh, no, you're not." Carrie jumped off the bed and barred the door to the hallway, her arms dramatically outstretched. "No way! I won't let you throw away—"

"Carrie!" Suddenly Shelley was furious, not at her friend so much, but at fate, the world, everything that seemed to be conspiring to make her miserable. "It's not up to you. It's my life." She glared at Carrie, eyes blazing. "Did I interfere when Jim left for Peru and you wouldn't go with him? Did I tell you what a mistake I thought you were making? No. I left it up to you to handle your own life. Please have the courtesy to allow me the same freedom."

Carrie seemed to crumple before her eyes, and remorse shot through Shelley. She leaped forward and threw her arms around her friend. "Oh, Carrie, I'm so sorry. I shouldn't have brought your marriage into this. It's not fair."

"No." Carrie gently disentangled herself from Shelley's embrace and walked unsteadily toward the balcony. The breeze from the open doorway ruffled her shiny brown hair. "No, you were right. I can't make you do what I think you ought to, any more than you can make me." Her sigh was long and painful. "And now that it's out in the open, how about leveling with me? What do you think about the mess I've made of my life?"

"Carrie, this is hardly the time or the place—"

"Please, Shelley." She turned and looked into her friend's face. "Was it so wrong what I did? Isn't marriage supposed to be a fifty-fifty proposition? Shouldn't he have met me halfway?"

Shelley hesitated. She felt like she was the last person in the world to be giving others advice right now. It wasn't as if she were doing such a wonderful job of her own relationship.

"That's the ideal situation, but not many people achieve it," she told Carrie at last. "You can't expect to go half and half on everything anyway. A marriage, or any other relationship, is the sum of all its parts. One partner may have to go three quarters of the way, or maybe even ninety percent now and then. You can't balance and weigh everything that way. It just doesn't work."

"So you think I should have given in to him. I should have gone to Peru."

Shelley took a deep breath. "I'm not saying that. Only you can say what your marriage was worth to you. I can't." She closed her eyes. "But when you love someone, really love them, you should be able to go the extra distance," she said softly, more to herself than to Carrie. "It all depends on what you can bear to do. Sometimes you have to stretch yourself."

How far could she stretch? Shelley asked herself. How far could Michael? They'd have to be a pair of contortionists to make anything work between the two of them. No, it was impossible.

Carrie began to pace the floor of the hotel room. Suddenly she chuckled, though the sound was harsh. "Do you know one of the reasons I was so hot on coming here to this resort? I thought I might meet a man who would wipe Jim out of my mind." She laughed a humorless gurgle and walked out onto the balcony. "That's what I wanted to do—to prove to myself that there were more where Jim came from, that I could always find a man."

When Shelley came out beside her, she saw the tears slowly sliding down her friend's tanned cheeks, and silently she put an arm around her shoulders and drew her near.

"I found men all right. Tons of them. Of every size and shape and personality." A sob broke her sentence. "But not one of them was Jim. He's the only man I'll ever love. I know that now. And I've let him slip away."

"It's not too late . . ."

"It is. I was so angry that he would take that job in Peru without consulting me, I told him I wouldn't go with him. We both put up the barricades, fighting about it every day. And then, suddenly, he was gone. And I was so—so alone."

"Carrie, I'm sure he still loves you . . ."

"I'm not so sure. The last letter I got asked if I'd

filed for divorce yet. That was all. Not even 'How are you, do you miss me?' "

"He's still hurt."

Carrie turned and hugged Shelley hard. "So am I," she said, sobbing, her voice muffled by tears and Shelley's shoulder.

"Let's get out of here," Shelley said. "I think we both need to go home."

Carrie nodded. "I'll start packing."

"And I'll write a letter to Michael." She smiled at Carrie's tear-stained face. "We'll go home and have a real talk, okay? And we'll figure out a way to show Jim how sorry you are about what happened."

Carrie gave her a wavery smile. "Sure. Why not? Miracles have happened before."

Miracles, Shelley thought as she hurried back to Michael's room to collect her things. Maybe that was what she needed. But didn't they only happen to angels?

Too bad old girl, she told herself. Looks like you're out of luck.

Eight

"The purpose of Assertiveness Training is to teach you to take charge of your life. To do this you must be able to set your own goals and map ways of working toward them." That was what the book said.

"Fine." Shelley slapped the book down on her desk after reading the paragraph over eleven times. "That's exactly what I'll do."

She took out a blank sheet of paper and began writing.

Goal 1. Forget about Michael Harper.

Goal 2. Focus on your work.

Goal 3. Divorce emotions from your professional life.

She bit the end of her pencil. It was no use. She wasn't going to be able to do any of those things until she found out what had happened to Michael that day in Newport.

She and Carrie had left in a hurry. She'd scribbled out a letter to Michael, full of poorly thought out arguments against seeing him again—things like "The cliché that opposites attract has always been a fallacy" and "You spend your days seeking physical danger while I spend mine trying to alleviate the emotional danger in people's lives—you walk the razor's edge by choice, I try to pull people like you back from the brink" and ending with "Please don't try to contact me in any way."

And he hadn't. If she looked down into her heart of hearts, she had to admit that had surprised her, and maybe even hurt her a little. Not one letter, one visit, one phone call. He might have disappeared off the face of the earth for all she knew.

So you see, she scolded herself often, what you did was exactly right. He didn't really care a thing about you. You were a fun challenge for a slow day in Newport. Other than that, you were certainly expendable.

But in the back of her mind one question kept nagging at her: What happened when he confronted Harry Stickler? Had there been shots fired? Had he been hit?

Four days had passed since the weekend. Michael hadn't kept his weekly appointment with Jerry. So where was he? What had happened?

Assertiveness training be damned, she had to find out! When she finally admitted that to herself, adrenaline flooded her body, and she jumped into action, dialing the number on the form he'd filled out in Jerry's office.

"The number you have dialed has been disconnected," the robotlike tone of the recording informed her.

So much for the direct approach. There was still the office he worked for. She looked up the number of the district attorney's office and rang it.

"Michael Harper?" the switchboard operator asked. "I have no listing for that name."

Of course not. Undercover operators had unlisted numbers. Now what? Shelley stared at the Mary Cassatt print for a long time before she could make herself take the next step. Then she pulled on a jacket and ran out into the parking lot and got into her car for the drive to the station house.

It wasn't long before she was standing at the door to Detective Sam Gladstone's office. "Detective Gladstone? May I speak with you for a moment?"

He leaned back in his chair, his long, lean body alert. She could see that he didn't quite recognize her at first, but by the time he'd nodded his acquiescence, the memories had been stirred to life.

"Dr. Pride, isn't it?"

"I'm not a doctor yet," she said automatically, coming in slowly to stand before his desk.

"Sit down." He rose and offered her a chair. "What can I do for you?"

She dropped into the chair and smiled nervously. Just what *could* he do for her? Shelley wondered. That was the hard part. How was she going to get through this without looking like an idiot?

"Detective, we met a few weeks ago under unusual circumstances. . . ."

His dark face almost smiled. "Not so unusual for me," he reminded her.

"Oh, no, of course not." She slid forward on her chair. "But it was for me. I was a witness against a Michael Harper. You seemed to know him fairly well."

He nodded solemnly. He wasn't about to make this any easier. She was going to have to go all the way on her own.

"I . . . I wonder if you could give me some information about Mr. Harper. Have you seen him lately? In the last few days?"

His gaunt face showed no hint of what he was thinking. "I'm sorry, Ms. Pride. Michael Harper has no official connection to the police department. There's nothing I can tell you about him."

"Can you just tell me if you've seen him since the weekend?"

He shook his head. "I'm sorry."

Did that mean Yes, but I can't tell you about it; or No, I haven't seen him; or Yes, I've seen him and he was in horrible shape. Who knew what the man was saying! He wasn't about to give away a thing.

She rose from her seat, anger alternating with regret. "I don't suppose you could give me any idea where I might go to look for him?"

He'd think she was "mad about the boy," wouldn't he? That she had a crush on him and wanted to look him up. Well, he wouldn't be far off at that. And who cared what he thought anyway?

"I'm sorry," he said again.

She turned to leave, but at the doorway of his office, she paused. This was her last hope. If he wouldn't help her, the only thing left to do was wander the streets and hope to run into Michael by accident somewhere. Pretty bad odds there. She turned back, determined. If she had to tell him everything in order to find out about Michael, she'd do it.

"Listen, Mr. Gladstone, I know you think it's sort of odd, my trying to find out about Michael."

This time he really did grin. "Not at all. You'd be surprised at how many attractive young ladies want to know all about Michael."

She answered his smile reluctantly. "I don't think I'd be surprised at all. But . . ." She slipped back down into the chair. "Let me tell you why I'm asking. You see, I ran into Michael this weekend in

Newport. He was—on assignment, if you know what I mean. And we kind of—ended up together."

How much could she really tell him? Not the details of the case Michael was on. But he knew what Michael did for a living.

"When I left him, he was going to some sort of showdown. He"—she took a deep breath—"he was wearing a gun. And when I didn't hear from him again, I got so worried." She leaned across the desk and looked at him beseechingly. "Please tell me he's all right, if you know anything at all about him."

His eyes were actually twinkling. Probably he was laughing at the silly besotted female, but she didn't care. It was worth it if she got information.

"It seems to me I warned you about this very thing," he said slowly.

"What?" She wasn't sure what he was talking about.

"I seem to remember telling you that it was all right to trust Michael with your afternoon, but not your life."

"Oh." Yes, she remembered. But what did that have to do with anything? "Well, I haven't. Trusted him with my life, I mean." She felt color creeping into her cheeks. "What I mean is, I really wouldn't want him to know I was asking about him this way. I told him not to try to see me again when I left Newport. But then I started worrying about the gun. . . ."

"Men like Michael," he went on, leaning toward her and talking as though she hadn't said a word, "crave the excitement of the new and different. They can't stand repetition. Pastoral scenes bore them to tears. They don't make good husbands."

"Detective Gladstone." Shelley drew herself up. "I know all that. I didn't come for a lecture in relationship adjustment. I just want to know if Michael is all right."

He grimaced. "I don't know."

He might, or he might not, be telling the truth. He looked so cold and unbending, sitting there. Didn't he have any heart at all? Shelley stared at him for a long, fruitless moment, then gave up. "All right, Detective. Sorry to have taken your time." She rose and started for the door again. She was almost through it when he spoke.

"I'll see what I can find out, Ms. Pride. Leave me your number. I'll get in touch with you."

Funny how a moment before he'd looked cold and heartless, and now, despite his lean physique, he seemed like Santa Claus. She danced out of the station and drove back to her office in a haze. That night when the phone rang at about nine o'clock, she knew before she answered it that it was going to be news about Michael.

"He's in Hawaii," Sam Gladstone told her. "There were some loose ends to a case he was working on over the weekend that took him there."

"So he's all right?" Shelley closed her eyes with relief. "Thank God," she whispered.

"He seems to be fine." There was a pause. "One other thing."

"Yes?" Something in his voice told her this "other thing" was not going to be pleasant.

"He may be staying."

"In Hawaii?" She felt numb.

"Yes. There's an opening in an organization he's been interested in for a long time. They've offered him the job. Rumor is, he's accepted."

"I see." It doesn't matter, she was saying to herself over and over, like a chant, a mantra. It doesn't matter, it doesn't matter.

But it did matter. She couldn't fool herself. He was so far away. She felt sick inside at the thought of the ocean between them. *I'll never see him again,* she thought. *How can I stand it?*

"Thank you so much, Detective. I really do appreciate it."

She hung up the telephone feeling as though a cement mixer had taken up residence in her stomach.

There was one thing about being a psychologist—she had a thousand and one remedies for what ailed her, all lining the walls of her office, all safely ensconced in the books that she'd read and studied for years. She could pull almost any title from the shelf and know it contained a confident prescription for putting her life in order.

But even though she tried, none of the usual answers worked for her the next morning. She saw the few clients on her schedule and was able to keep her mind on their problems for the required hour. She even gave them each some good suggestions on improving their own attitudes—and felt like a hypocrite the whole time. How did she dare tell these people what to do when she couldn't take her own advice?

It was all for the best, she kept telling herself. The farther away he was, the easier to forget him.

But why hadn't he at least given her a call? a little traitorous voice, deep inside, kept carping. Why didn't he drop you a postcard? *Love the islands, wish you were here.*

Because he's forgotten all about you, silly. Because he's having the time of his life, and you were but a moment in an eternity of excitement. Face it, and get on with things.

Okay. That's what I'll do. In just a little while. First, let me remember his dark hair, and the eyes that sparkled like stars and the way his hand would slip down to cover my shoulder with warmth. . . .

By late afternoon she knew she had to do something. Transactional Analysis might be an answer. It was, after all, an approach she'd been getting into lately. Why wasn't she using it? It was time to forget the Child in herself and bring out the Adult. "Act happy, and you'll be happy," she told herself, just as she'd told others so many times. "Go through the motions and eventually they become reality for you."

Michael was out of her life. She should be happy about that. It was what she wanted, what she'd asked for. So why wasn't she celebrating?

She took care of that on the way home from work. Stopping at the most exclusive market in town, she bought three thick steaks, a pair of tall candles, and a bottle of golden champagne. "I'm going to celebrate until I'm happy," she told herself through clenched teeth. "No matter how long it takes."

The apartment had a still, expectant air to it as she let herself in with the key. "Carrie?" she called out, heading straight into the kitchen by way of the hall, completely bypassing the living room. "We're going to have a party. I'm even planning to invite good old Jerry. What do you think?"

Silence greeted her. She put her grocery bags on the counter and began to unpack them, thinking Carrie must be out until she heard the door from the dining area open behind her.

"Shelley." Carrie's voice was strained.

Shelley turned and looked at her friend. "What's the matter? You look as though you'd seen a ghost."

"Shelley, Michael's here."

She whirled, turning away from the door just as it was opening again. Staring at the stove, she kept pulling things out of the paper bag blindly with no idea what she was moving from one place to another. She could feel him in the room. Every part of her was screaming with the need to turn and run to him, but she wouldn't let herself do it. Instead, she pulled out the three steaks and placed them on the counter, tearing off the white paper, then reached into the bag again.

"Hello, Shelley." His voice was low and rich, just as she remembered it.

Her fingers tightened on the loaf of bread she'd just pulled from the sack, holding on as though it were a life preserver. He really was all right, and he was here, and any moment now, she was going to have to turn and face him. Would he read the truth in her eyes? Anything—anything but that!

"Hi, Michael." Pretend he was Jerry or any other man she knew casually—that was the answer. Turn and grin at him as you would at any drop-in guest. She turned slowly, a false smile plastered on her lips. "What are you doing here?"

The smile hadn't been plastered well enough. It fell away fast once she got a good look at him. Who was this person in her kitchen? The first Michael Harper she'd met had been suave and elegantly dressed. Mike Daniels had been a little tackier, but nothing to startle the birds out of trees. But this! Atop black hair slicked back with enough grease to lubricate half the cars in the county sat huge dark glasses, poised at an arrogant angle. He wore a scuffed-up black leather jacket over a soiled T-shirt, dirty jeans that clung to his thighs like snakeskin, and boots. To top it off his handsome face was obscured by a two-day growth of beard that made him appear about as cuddly as a Harley-Davidson. And with all that he still looked so good to her, she felt her stomach fall away at the sight of him.

"What on earth?" She gestured toward his outfit.

"Don't you like this?" He posed, tough guy. "I

thought it made me look like early Marlon Brando. What do you think? Am I cool, or what?"

His eyes were laughing and suddenly so was she. "I can dig it," she said. "Like, you're really hip, Daddy-o."

"Like, thanks, baby." He sidled up to her and spoke out of the corner of his mouth. "Like, you wanna go for a ride on my chopped hog?" He bobbed his eyebrows at her suggestively, and she was laughing at him, loving him helplessly, until she noticed Carrie backing out of the kitchen door, trying to escape.

"Carrie!" she called out, suddenly desperate. She couldn't be alone with Michael. He'd have her completely under control in no time at all. He was already halfway there.

"Gotta go." Carrie waved, looking guilty. "Just remembered an errand I've gotta run. See you in an hour or so." And she was gone.

"Smart girl, your roommate," Michael said, leaning back against the counter and tilting his head to gaze at her. "Bet she'd go for a ride on my cycle if I asked her."

"I'll bet she wouldn't." Shelley turned back to look at him. Everything inside was bubbling with uneasy confusion. She gripped the bread even harder. "Why are you wearing that ridiculous outfit?"

"I'm working." He broke a stalk off the bunch of celery she'd set on the counter and began to chew the end of it.

"What are you doing, infiltrating the Hell's Angels?"

His blue eyes were bright and steady. "This is one case I'm not going to let you get involved in," he told her softly, "so I don't think I'll answer that."

She licked her lips nervously. He was acting as though they'd just said good-bye yesterday, as though he hadn't told her to wait for him and then come back to find her gone. Had he even read the letter? Maybe he'd never gone back to the hotel room himself. With a sinking heart she realized she might have to go through all the explanations again, and this time to his face.

"Michael, about the other day . . ."

He was gazing at her steadily and she couldn't find much humor in his eyes. "Are you referring to the morning, when we made love, or to the evening, when you skipped out on me?"

So he did know. "Did you read the letter I left for you? It explained—"

"Letter?" He pretended to look blank. "I don't remember any letter. There were some incoherent rantings scratched on the back of an old envelope. Something about divergent careers and lack of mutual interests. I didn't pay any attention to that."

Why was her heart beating so fast? She had to get hold of herself. "You should pay some attention to it, Michael. I meant every word." Her eyes were flashing. "And that wasn't some old envelope. It was hotel stationery. I didn't have anything else."

He shrugged, biting off another chunk of celery. "Whatever. It doesn't matter."

She squeezed the bread. "It does too matter," she announced evenly.

"No." He looked at her through narrowed eyes. "I know a little psychology, too, you know. I can tell when a woman is just putting up barriers to make the chase more exciting."

Her jaw dropped with outrage and she squeezed the bread even harder. "What? You egotistical—"

"I see you have a new hobby," he interrupted, pointing to the tortured loaf she was still clinging to. "Abstract sculptures, is it? And using bread putty to make them. What an ingenious idea." His grin was back. "What does that shape represent?"

She looked down at it in disgust. "Your neck," she shot back, giving the loaf a vicious twist. She tossed the soggy mass into the trash and turned back to him. "Now, listen, Michael. We've got to talk."

"Absolutely." He threw down the rest of his stalk of celery and suddenly she was in his arms. "But first we've got to make out a little."

Even in the rough ensemble he wore, his body felt hard and clean, and she wanted to reach inside the jacket and run her hands across his muscular chest. How tempting it was to take a bit of his warmth to her again! She had to resist if she was going to keep her sanity.

"No!" She struggled against his embrace. "I don't want to 'make out'!"

"That's just the way we motorcycle guys talk," he said, talking tough again and nibbling on her neck. "If you're not up for making out, how about we get right down to a little petting? We talk about that too." His hand slipped under her cashmere sweater and began to rub gently against one stiffening nipple.

Somehow her struggle had turned very quickly into something that more closely resembled a snuggle. How did he always manage to do this to her? "Michael!" She was beginning to feel drugged. "Stop it!"

"Such rebellion," he murmured near her ear. "How did I seduce you before? What was my secret?" He chuckled. "I remember now. Food jokes."

"Oh no, please. . . ." Despite herself the laughter was welling up again.

"Let's see now. Oh, I've got one." He licked her ear lobe and cupped her breast with his large hand. "You know what ghosts eat for breakfast, don't you?"

"Michael." She tried to make it sound like an ominous warning, but she failed. Naturally.

"Dreaded wheat, of course." He shook his head. "I'm amazed you didn't know that one."

"Oh, Michael." She gave in and smiled. "You tell the most awful jokes."

He raised an eyebrow wickedly. "Watch out or I'll tell you the one about the world-famous chef who had to give up making his prize-winning soufflé when his wife left him. He found he just couldn't make it without her."

He leaned back and looked into her face. "Just like me," he said huskily. "I'm beginning to realize I can't make it without you either. So cut out this talk of incompatibility, would you?"

What was he saying? She stared at him, too stunned to resist when he kissed her, then too confused. Was he saying he loved her? That he wanted to be with her forever?

No, stupid, what was left of her rational side scolded. He's only saying he wants to be with you until the excitement dulls and he's ready to move on to find a new place with more thrills.

But even those doubts faded as his incredible warmth flooded her, taking over like a hot desert wind, sweeping through her body, through her emotions, laying waste to all her defenses.

She was in her own kitchen with Michael's arms around her, Michael's mouth on hers, but she felt as though she might have been on the edge of an Arizona mesa—hair streaming behind her, head thrown back, body stretched like a bow, welcoming the rush of the hot wind as it sped over the burning red sands and came to curl around her body.

What she felt for Michael was like that: a force of nature more than an act of man. It overwhelmed her, swept her away, tossed her into dreams and fantasies she'd never experienced before. How sweet it would be to let that happen, to relax and sail along with that desert wind. But she couldn't allow that.

"Michael . . ." Somehow she'd ended up tight against him, inside his jacket, arms around his waist, her hands beneath his shirt, exploring his back. His flesh was slick and smooth and she wanted to run her hands down the length of him. She buried her face in his chest, breathing in the crisp male scent that came in a wave of warmth from his skin. She knew with sudden certainty that she would never feel for another man what she felt for this one.

"Don't bother me," he breathed against her neck. "I'm busy right now."

"We've got to talk." She struggled to get free, not sure if the major battle was with him, or with herself. "Please, Michael. Please."

He let her go reluctantly, his touch lingering on her breast, then her shoulder. "I don't think I'm going to like this talk," he grumbled as she led him to the kitchen table and sat across from him. "I can feel a real wave of logical thinking coming from your direction. I hate logical thinking."

How was she going to be able to sit here and look into those crystal-blue eyes and still get out what she had to say? "Michael," she began shakily, "why aren't you in Hawaii?"

"Hawaii?" Suddenly a strange thing happened. The face that had been so open, so full of humor, so loving, turned to a steel mask that she hardly recognized. She'd touched upon his work in a way he didn't like at all. Just seeing that transformation sent a distinct chill down Shelley's spine. "What are you talking about?"

She looked down at her hands. "I know you've been in Hawaii."

"Where did you find that out?" His voice was as sharp as the blade of a knife, and when she looked up, his eyes were cold as glacial ice.

That must be the man criminals see when the time comes to reveal who he is, Shelley thought, wide-eyed. She wouldn't want to tangle with him if he ever really got angry. Thank goodness there was nothing to hide here. "Sam Gladstone told me. I—I happened to see him at the station house the other day. . . ."

"And he just blurted it out?" He didn't believe that for a minute, but at least the ice had melted. He didn't feel threatened by her knowing anymore. Sam Gladstone's name seemed to work wonders. "Sure, he did." He grinned. "Come on, Shelley. Sam wouldn't tell a thing like that to a casual visitor. It wasn't for general knowledge."

She certainly wasn't going to admit what she'd gone through to find out. "I asked him," she said quickly. "I was wondering how that case with Harry Stickler came out, and I just asked him. And—he told me." Was he going to buy it?

"Give me a break."

Nope. What was she going to do now?

"I know Sam a little better than that." He narrowed his eyes at her with mock menace. "You must have batted those big brown eyes like crazy to charm old Sam into giving away my secrets."

She lifted her chin proudly. "I didn't have to bat anything. I just presented my side with reason and he told me what he knew."

He reached out so fast, she didn't have time to draw away, and then he had her wrist in his hand. "Then tell me this, lady shrink. Why would a woman who'd professed to want nothing more to do with me go to that kind of trouble to find out where I was?"

There was no logical answer to that question.

"Just crazy, I guess," she said instead of answering seriously. "But that's not the point."

"It may not be your point," he said pleasantly, "but it's exactly mine."

She took a very deep breath and held it for a long moment. "Michael, listen to me. I'm a psychologist. I'm developing a clinical practice. I love what I do. I've studied all my life for this. I'm a settled, conservative kind of person."

He nodded. "So far, I follow you."

"You live a very different sort of life. You're here today, gone tomorrow. You follow excitement, wherever it leads. You thrive on taking chances. You"—her voice dropped almost to a whisper—"you scare me. I don't think I can deal with that kind of constant risk. The worry." She swallowed hard. "And most of all, the fear that you'll be gone when I get up in the morning."

She'd expected him to rebut everything she said, but he fooled her again. He slowly let go of her wrist, not saying a word. When she met his eyes again, his glance was somber.

"You really lay it on the line, don't you?" he said quietly. "You look ahead in ways I don't usually do." He sighed. "What can I tell you, Shelley? I can't promise you white lace and a double-ring ceremony. Not with the way I live."

That was just what she knew was true, but it still hurt. Maybe a little piece of her heart had hoped to hear him declare his wild life over—that he would give up anything and everything to have her. But she knew how unrealistic that was. At least he didn't lie.

"That doesn't mean I don't want you." He reached out again and took both her hands in his. His eyes were dark and infinitely blue. "And you're not the only one who's scared," he said softly, looking at her as though that should mean something significant.

But what did it mean? *You've got to tell me,* she wanted to say aloud. *I'm a little too dense to get this from hints. If you want me to know something, you've got to tell me right out. Otherwise I'll never believe it.*

But he didn't say another word, so she ventured another question. "Are you going to take the job in Hawaii?"

"I didn't realize Sam was such a blabbermouth." He shook his head. "I'm not taking it."

"Why not?"

He dismissed it with a shrug. "You're not in Hawaii," he said simply. "And I want to be where you are."

Could it be possible? They hardly knew each other. And yet she knew it was. She felt that way about him. That's why she knew she had to stay away. Didn't he realize she was doing this as much for his sake as for her own? Didn't he remember how he'd told her that an emotional relationship would make him vulnerable in his work? She couldn't risk being the cause of his getting hurt.

"You can't," she told him. "I'm not going to see you."

He sighed, let go of her hands, and leaned back in the chair. "I was afraid you were going to make this difficult."

"Not difficult," she told him sadly. "Impossible."

The front door opened. Carrie was back. "I'm home," she called unnecessarily from the other room. "How come I don't smell those steaks on the grill?"

Michael stood and came close to where Shelley was sitting. "I've got news for you, Shelley," he said softly, cupping her chin in his hand and tilting her head up so that she had to look into his eyes. "You and I belong together. I had a feeling that was the way it was going to be from the first, but after our night in Newport I was sure of it. You're my lady. It's going to take some time to convince you of this, I know. But I've had tougher cases." He grinned. "None I cared more about winning, however. And like the Canadian Mounties, I always get my—woman."

Carrie chose that moment to breeze into the room. "Hi, guys. Michael staying for dinner?" she asked hopefully. "I bet he'd like one of those steaks."

"No," Shelley and Michael both answered at the same time, though each for different reasons.

"I'm working," Michael said, still looking down at Shelley. "I've got to get back on the job." Leaning down, he dropped a quick kiss on her unresisting lips. "But I will take this along with me." Turning, he grabbed a fork and stabbed one of the steaks, thrusting it into the empty paper sack.

"What do you want that for?" Shelley asked, frowning as she rose from her chair.

He waved the paper bag under her nose. "I heard what you said when you first came in. I'm not letting 'good old Jerry' have anything that belongs to me." He gave her a piercing look. "Nor anyone else, for that matter." He softened his words with a smile at Carrie. "See you later," he told them both before disappearing out the door, the sack with the steak held firmly in hand.

Shelley stood frozen to the spot.

"Shelley," Carrie said tentatively, moving toward her, "is there anything—"

"Not now." Shelley threw her a look that was desperate and apologetic at the same time. "I can't talk about it now." And she fled to her bedroom.

You're my lady, he'd said. How she longed to be just that! But it was impossible. For his own good as well as hers. How was she going to convince him of that?

Nine

"It was that vacation weekend in Newport." Carrie sighed, hand to forehead in dramatic anguish. "Too much sun. It's addled your brain."

"Carrie," Shelley warned, holding her coffee mug as though it were a cup of brandy on a snowy plain, and the only thing between life and frostbite. "I'm counting on you to help me."

Carrie sat across the kitchen table, shaking her head. "Would a true friend help you to ruin your life?"

"Would a true friend help me ruin Michael's?" Shelley had tried to explain to Carrie, giving her as much information about what Michael did as she dared.

Carrie frowned. "I'm not sure I buy this business of his loving you ruining his concentration and dedication. It sounds fishy to me. I still say you're running away from something."

Shelley took a long sip of coffee. She couldn't be

angry at Carrie. She knew her friend was only thinking of her happiness. But it would be so much easier if she would just accept what had to be done and agree to follow along. "You can say whatever you like. But please, please, help me the way I've asked."

"Ah, yes. Shall we go over it again?" At least Carrie seemed to be resigned to the plan. "When letters arrive in the mail I'm to write 'refused' and send them back. When he calls on the phone, I'm to tell him you won't speak to him. When he arrives at the door, as he will"—she shook a warning finger at Shelley—"I'm to tell him you won't see him, that you aren't home, that you don't ever want to see him again, that you've taken a seat on the next Space Shuttle and won't be back until 1999, that you've changed your name and dyed your hair . . ."

"Thank you, Carrie." Shelley stemmed the flow of words and gave her a plastic smile. "I'm so glad you're getting into the spirit of this."

"We aim to please." Carrie bounced up out of her seat and took her own mug to the sink. "I'm going to run down and check the mail right now." She waved as she swung out the door. "And don't worry. If there's anything from Michael, I won't let it get anywhere near this apartment."

Shelley sighed, listening to the door slam shut. She knew that what she was doing was for the best. If only she could explain it so that others would understand.

But Carrie wasn't in much of a mood to understand anything right now. She'd finally come to a decision and sent a letter to Jim two days before, asking if she could please join him in Peru.

"It isn't as if I had a career here, or anything like that," she'd said convincing herself as she was writing it. The two of them had been in the living room. Shelley was working on a case report and

Carrie was pacing back and forth in front of the stereo, changing records as her mercurial mood switched gears. And every now and then she stopped at the table to add another sentence to the letter she was writing.

"I'm a legal secretary, but I can do secretarial work anywhere," she declared, stopping in front of the chair where Shelley was sitting. "Why didn't I look at it that way when he first told me about the job in South America?" She shook her head, bewildered. "I was so caught up in what was fair and what wasn't. I didn't look at it from his point of view. And so I threw him away to stand on a principle."

"You'll make it up to him when you get there," Shelley had comforted her confidently.

"If he still wants me," Carrie'd answered softly. She'd sunk to the floor and closed her eyes. "Oh, please, make him still want me."

And so she'd sent off the message, and now she was racing to the mailbox every half hour to see if there was a reply, even though her outgoing letter had hardly had time to clear the runway at Los Angeles International Airport yet.

Despite her misgivings, Carrie would be true to her word and help Shelley persuade Michael to give up on their romance. And for the next two days the plan seemed to work. Michael called only once, and when Carrie told him that Shelley wouldn't speak to him, he sounded almost cheerful.

"I'd watch out if I were you," Carrie crowed, enjoying it immensely. "He's going to come into your room like a cat burglar or drop off the side of a building on you. Just you wait. He won't take this lying down."

Shelley spent a nervous night with her window locked and an uneasy day glancing up at lampposts and rooftops, but there was no sign of Michael. She'd almost forgotten about Carrie's warning by the time she left work for the library the next day. She had some research to do for her lecture series, and she was absorbed in thinking about her topic when she drove up to the tree-shaded public library. She didn't notice the car that drove up and parked behind her.

She did see Michael once she was inside, however. He kept showing up at the other side of the stacks she was browsing through. He didn't say anything—just winked, then sauntered away. And she dropped a book every time, or knocked over a whole row of them. Her nerves were jumping at every turn.

Then he disappeared. She caught sight of him a little later, leaning against the circulation desk, flirting with the young librarian. She walked right by him to check out her books. The clerk chatted amiably as she went about the stamping and checking, but Shelley's attention was all on the couple standing a few feet away.

It was revolting to listen to other people flirt. She felt her nails digging into her palms, and she was furious with herself for caring, furious with him for showing her that she did. She marched out with her head held high, then had to go back for the books she'd forgotten on the counter. He never made a move toward her and she hated him for that too.

Maybe he was just there through coincidence, she told herself. Maybe he was showing her that he no longer cared about dating her. But she knew that couldn't be true. And the next evening he proved it.

She'd stopped at the local supermarket to pick up a few things for dinner. It never occurred to her that he would corner her there. She'd just reached out and picked up a long loaf of crusty French bread when the voice behind her made her jump into the air.

"Stocking up on more bread putty, I see. In for a big evening of bread sculpture, are you?"

She whirled. She was ready for him. She was going to be dignified and to the point, and most important she was not going to laugh, no matter how he provoked her. "Don't do this, Michael. Please."

"Do what?" He spread his arms wide in total innocence. "I'm just shopping for groceries like everyone else." He pointed out the wire cart parked behind hers. "Look at this. One quart of milk. A pound of linguine. Evidence." He smiled smugly.

Raking him with a scathing glance, she looked suspiciously into the cart. "What are you planning to do with that can of baby formula?" she asked.

"Baby formula?" He looked down at it, coughed, and shuffled his feet. "Would you believe my cousin just came in from Phoenix to stay with me, bringing baby and all? Cute little bugger. Hope you get to meet them someday."

She met his gaze firmly. "I wouldn't believe anything of the kind," she said with pleasant contradiction.

Just then a young woman with a baby strapped to her chest came up and wheeled the cart away, baby formula and all. They both watched her go, Shelley with triumph, Michael with regret.

"Your cousin's not too friendly, is she?" Shelley commented.

"Uh . . . laryngitis. That's it." He nodded wisely. "She can't talk and she's rather shy about it. . . ." He raised his eyebrows. "You're not buying this, are you?" he asked sadly.

"Not for a moment."

Sighing, he tried to take her elbow, though she managed to evade him. "Oh, well. It was worth a try." He could see that she wasn't anywhere near cracking under his inept campaign of deceit, so he quickly changed tactics. "I'll go and get a shopping cart so I can be a real shopper, just like you. Stay here. Don't run away."

Don't run away. She was rooted to the spot. She watched him stride quickly toward the rack where the shopping carts were corraled. He was dressed simply in dark slacks and a crisp blue shirt, but he caused a small sensation nonetheless. Heads turned as he passed, and admiring female glances followed him everywhere he went, Shelley noted. He was so good-looking. He made her melt inside. Did he do that to everyone?

A wave of tension tightened through her. He was too good-looking for his own good. Undercover agents were supposed to be dull, bland, forgettable people, Shelley told herself. Michael was definitely noticeable and absolutely memorable. Wasn't that dangerous? Shouldn't she warn him?

Her hands clenched on the handle of the shopping cart. Stop it, she ordered herself. You're either in his life or you aren't. You can't have it both ways. And what are you doing standing here, waiting for him, just as he told you to?

Turning, she pushed her cart purposefully down the aisle, making a sharp turn just beyond the ice cream and then a left that put her right in front of the soup display. It was going to take him a while to find her here.

Feeling pleased with herself for her evasive maneuvers, she began to peruse the soup cans. She didn't need much, after all. She'd just grab a few cans of cream of mushroom, dash through the produce section to pick up salad makings, and be out of here in no time.

"Think a nice bowl of chicken noodle would help soothe my wounded ego?"

She jumped. "Why do you always sneak up on me like that?"

He shook his head. "I'm not sneaking. You're just not paying me the proper attention."

He was so adorable, Shelley thought. His dark hair was slightly ruffled, falling over his forehead in a way that made him look young and vulnerable.

Vulnerable? Who was she kidding? This man had the skin of a rhinoceros! She was going to have to get tough.

"Michael," she said sternly, trying to frown. "You've got to stop following me around." She was prepared to go into an extensive lecture on the right of privacy, but he didn't give her the chance.

"Who, me?" He looked aghast, as though she'd accused him of some horrible crime, then he looked about him as though to gather support from the passing shoppers. "I'm not following you around. I'm just shopping, like everybody else. I should be allowed to stop and chat with a pretty fellow shopper who happens to stumble across my path." He pointed into his cart. "Look. Real food. And I picked it myself this time."

His "real food" consisted of a large bag of gooey doughnuts and a six-pack of beer.

"What's that?" she asked distastefully .

"Dinner," he answered.

"You'll get sick," she accused. "You can't live on that junk."

"I know." His eyes were baby-wide. "I need someone to take care of me."

"Oh, Michael." She was going to laugh if she didn't get out of here. Picking up three cans of soup at random, she tossed them into her basket and began to march down the aisle, pushing her cart in front of her, on her way to the produce section. Michael, of course, was right behind her.

Don't speak to him, she advised herself silently. Don't look at him. Don't answer if he talks. Don't love him, a tiny voice added mournfully toward the end. But that was obviously a lost cause.

"These carts are pretty neat, aren't they?" His cheery voice came from right behind her shoulder blades. "I bet we could get up some fantastic races if we got all the shoppers together. We could assign handicaps according to age and conditioning, filling up the carts with groceries depending upon the numbers." He managed to maneuver himself right alongside her as they came up into the vegetables. "I think I'd insist you carry a nice big turkey in yours," he teased.

"Are you volunteering?" she snapped back, then groaned. He'd gotten to her again.

"Oh-ho. She's got a wicked temper after all." He grinned happily.

Shelley picked up a ball of lettuce as though she were ready to lob it at his head. A sudden fantasy ripped through her mind. She'd throw the lettuce at Michael. He'd come back at her with a barrage of brussels sprouts. The whole section would erupt with flying food, everyone getting involved in the action, and she would escape through the produce man's entrance. She balanced the lettuce in her hand, biting her lip. It was a tempting thought. To stay here this way was madness. The food riot seemed like sanity in comparison.

"Did anyone ever tell you that the freckles on your nose dance when you're angry?"

Anger was her only defense. Somehow she managed to frown again. "This isn't fair, Michael. You know you're taking advantage here. I wish you'd leave me alone."

"Sorry." He popped a juicy cherry tomato into his mouth. "Can't do that. All's fair in love and war, and I'm fighting for my life here, you know."

His tone was light, but his eyes were full of meaning. Shaken, she turned to the produce bin and began shoveling mushrooms into a plastic bag.

"You know what the girl mushroom said to the boy mushroom?" he asked softly, picking up two of the little vegetables and holding them out. "You're a real fun guy."

She kept on shoveling, eyes slightly blurred by moisture. It wasn't working. She was going to give in to him. She could feel it coming.

"Don't you get it? Fungus-fungi?" He threw the mushrooms into her bag. "She gets it," he said as though talking to himself. "She just doesn't like it, fool." He sighed. "Time to work on a new approach."

Suddenly his hands were on her shoulders, turning her. "I'm going now," he informed her. "I'm off to lick my wounds and ready myself to return and face the slings and arrows of your scorn. . . ."

"Outrageous fortune," she corrected automatically, hardly hearing what he was saying. She kept her eyes downcast so he wouldn't see them filling with tears. His hands felt so strong and warm on her shoulders. She felt herself melting again.

"What?"

"Slings and arrows of outrageous fortune," she repeated, blinking away the moisture.

"Listen, doll," he said in his thickest Bogart imitation yet. "It's my quotation, I'll mess it up my way." He chucked her under the chin, then glanced at his watch. "Gotta run. Duty calls. Take care of these for me, will you? We'll share them for breakfast someday." He took the sack of doughnuts and six-pack of beer from his cart and placed them in hers. Then he turned and looked at her for a long moment. Eyes finally clear enough to risk meeting his, she looked up and found his gaze dark with real emotion. "I love you, Shelley," he said simply. "And I'm going to find a way to prove it to you."

The breath had stopped in her throat, but he

didn't know that. He was walking out through the supermarket, leaving her behind, leaning into the broccoli for support.

"I love you," he'd said, just like you told someone you liked his new haircut, or that you'd forgotten to send him a card on his birthday. Did he mean love, real love, the kind that lasted forever and cemented an attraction into a bond of oneness?

She was in turmoil again. She moved through the store like a sleepwalker, paying for the groceries and carrying them to her car without thinking. Was she wrong to keep him at bay? Was she really doing this for him? Was she too scared to face the truth?

"Garbanzo bean soup?" Carrie asked a few minutes later, back in the apartment, as she began pulling the cans from the bag. "Vegetarian herb broth?"

There was no point trying to explain to her roommate what had happened. "You've got to be open to new experiences, Carrie," she said instead, suddenly finding herself giggling with semihysteria. "Learn to try what scares you."

The next few days were a time of anarchy for Shelley. Her emotions were riding a roller coaster. One minute she was in the depths of despair, sure that it was insanity to love Michael; the next, she found herself grinning like a loon, happy just to think about him.

Carrie kept her distance, mostly eyeing Shelley from around corners, as though afraid whatever she had might be contagious. She still answered the phone whenever it rang, and checked on the mail, but when something finally did come from Michael, she couldn't bring herself to refuse it. Looking guilty as a naughty pup, she carried it in the front door.

"It says 'photograph enclosed'," she explained. "You can't send it back without taking a peek. We can steam it open and glue it back. He'll never know."

Shelley stared at the big manila envelope Carrie held out to her. She knew what she should do, but she also knew what she was going to do. Not letting herself think, she reached for it, ripped it open, and pulled out the picture.

There, in black and white splendor, was Michael, naked except for a very large maple leaf, strategically placed. The painted background was dismal, a godforsaken plain covered with burnt trees. There was a card attached. It said:

> Dear Shelley,
> This is how I feel without you. Naked and desolate. I'll make a solemn oath never to utter another food joke in your presence if you'll just promise to marry me on Sunday.
>
> Love,
> Michael
> P.S. What's your position on body-part puns?

She knew she'd been staring at the picture for much too long. That wasn't so bad really. It was the goofy smile she couldn't hold back that was embarrassing.

"I take it you don't want to send it back?" Carrie asked at last, and Shelley clutched it to her chest as though she were afraid Carrie might try to take it from her.

She couldn't speak. Mutely she shook her head, backing off to her bedroom.

"And we score another point for Michael's side," Carrie called out to no one in particular, but Shelley didn't pay any attention. She was in her room, staring at the picture, grinning again. For the first time she was able to study every gorgeous bit of Michael without any interference from anyone else. There was only one question that kept nagging at her. Who had taken the picture?

The reference to marriage didn't fool her. She knew he was joking. Men like Michael didn't get married, and she'd never even thought about it. No white lace and double-ring ceremony, he'd warned her. Well, she was beyond waiting for that. She'd run to him in a minute if . . . if she wasn't so scared.

Two days went by with no sign of Michael. That only confirmed her judgment. He was planning to drop in on her unexpectedly, she was sure. She had only to wait.

Carrie received a letter from the company Jim worked for in Peru. Jim had taken a leave of absence a week before her letter had arrived. No one knew exactly where he was. It was thought he might have taken a train trip to Brazil. He was due back by the end of the month. Did she want them to hold her letter until then, or send it back?

Carrie was just about at the end of her rope. "Brazil!" she'd wailed. "Isn't that where they have that beautiful white sand beach with all those bikinis? And Carnival? The girl from Ipanema? How am I going to compete with that?"

Shelley tried to comfort her, but she was inconsolable. "I'll bet he's met someone else." She sighed, lying back into the plush cushions of the couch. "I'll bet he took her to Brazil." Tears welled in her eyes. "Oh, Shelley, I've been such a fool!"

If Jim was off in the wilds of Brazil somewhere, there was no way they could contact him. The best thing Shelley could think of was to try to get Carrie's mind off her problems, at least for a while. Ignoring her objections, she bundled her up and took her to a movie and then out to eat Chinese food afterward. The food just about did the trick.

There was something about hot and sour soup and pan-fried dumplings that seemed to soothe Carrie's soul. By the time Shelley had her home, she was waxing philosophical about the whole affair.

And Shelley was wondering where Michael was. At the theater she'd watched with only one eye while the other was taking in the view of the other seats. While they ate behind tinkling bead curtains, she kept losing the train of conversation while she craned her neck, watching the door, sure that Michael would show up at any moment. But he hadn't.

And yet he would. It was only a matter of time. She was sure of it.

And she was right, but true to form, he caught her off-guard again. And once again, it was in the place she would least have expected him to find her. In fact, when she walked into the beauty parlor to have her monthly shampoo and cut, she'd felt as though she'd left a burden at the door. She was ready to relax, forget about everything else, and enjoy being pampered for an hour.

The shop was decorated with lots of wood and hanging plants. It was long and narrow, and at peak periods, such as today, eight operators were at work at once, creating enough beauty to flood the city.

"Come on back here," Nancy said, fastening the plastic bib that covered her from neck to knees. "I'll get you started on your shampoo right away."

She stretched out in the reclining chair, her head back in the sink, her eyes closed, and let her body float away as Nancy sprayed the warm water in her hair and began to rub in the slippery shampoo. It felt so good, so soothing, she didn't even pay attention when Nancy murmured something about being right back and left her there. It wasn't until Michael's voice came drifting in through her misty dream that she opened her eyes wide with shock and tried to sit up.

"Hello, lady shrink," he said softly. "Head-shrinking the easy way, aren't you? Does this count toward your degree?" He put a hand on her shoulder, keeping her down. "Uh-uh. Don't get up. You'll get soap in your eyes. Lie back. Trust me."

There really wasn't much choice. The chair was tilted back in a way that made it impossible for her to get up without doing something very awkward, like rolling onto the floor. So there she lay, blood rushing to her head, glaring up at Michael's smiling face.

"What are you doing here?" she hissed, hoping to get her dislike of his presence across without making a scene. "Where's Nancy?"

"Gone," he said cheerfully. "I'm taking over."

"What?" Despite the odds, she tried to rise again, only to be pushed back, firmly but gently, by her new shampoo person.

"Relax," he told her, and then his hands were on her head, and he was kneading the soap into her scalp.

"I don't believe this!" she cried, feeling utterly helpless. She knew what she must look like with her hair all wet and stringy, and the picture wasn't pretty. "Why are you doing this?"

"Nancy's going to be busy for a few minutes," he told her as though it were an everyday occurrence. "I volunteered to take over."

She looked up at him, wincing as he splashed fresh water in her hair that hit her eyes. "And she let you? Just like that?"

"Well . . ." He bent down and gave his captive audience a quick peck on the nose. "I sort of told her I knew what I was doing. That I'd studied under Saint Jacques in Quebec and knew all about the wedge cut and all that new stuff."

The kiss was very nice, sort of comforting, like the warm lick of a favorite spaniel. How could she stay angry with this man? "Who," she demanded, "is Saint Jacques?"

He shrugged. "You got me. I made it up. But she seemed impressed."

"Michael . . ." Oh, the hell with it! She was going to laugh if she wanted to! And laugh she did.

"Quiet," he told her with a mock frown. "You'll scandalize all the little ladies under the dryers. Just close your eyes and see if you like this."

What he did next was what should have scandalized all the little ladies under the dryers, if only they'd known just how heavenly his touch was on her unprotected head. Michael may not have studied under anyone named Saint Jacques, but he'd learned something somewhere.

His fingers moved strongly—rubbing, caressing, sifting through the thickness of her hair and finding every nerve ending she possessed. When she opened her eyes into little slits, all she could see was the sky-blue of his. When she closed them again, she could feel the warmth his fingers conjured up, and as all tension slowly fell away, a delicious tingling came to take its place. She felt him. She loved him. She wanted him with every part of her.

His touch was circling her ear, sending a tiny chain of chills across her, down her spine, down her legs. The little bubbles of the shampoo crackled like thunder in her ears, but she didn't notice. She was focused on Michael, and only Michael. Every sense was tuned to him, waiting to feel his command.

His fingers drew a line of sensation down her cheek, and she opened her eyes to meet his smile. His eyes were deep as mountain lakes. She wanted to plunge in, to draw him down on top of her, to roll with him in mountain meadows, crushing the wild flowers with their lovemaking.

"Like it?" he whispered.

She smiled, then let her lids drop sleepily again. More, she wanted to say. Much, much more.

But all too soon it was over. The warm water was cascading over her hair, rinsing out all the soap, and Michael was righting the chair so that she could finally come into a sitting position.

He put a towel over her head and she peeked out from under, suddenly shy to let him see her this way, without her dignity. "Where did Nancy go?" she asked. "What have you done with her?"

"I just sent her on a little errand," he said, taking her hand to lead her back to Nancy's booth. "She'll be right back."

"What did you do?" she asked suspiciously, sitting in the chair and turning it so she could look into his face. Michael was picking up a pair of scissors and experimenting, snapping them open and closed, and Shelley forgot all about Nancy for the moment.

"Oh, no, you don't," she said with firm conviction. "You may be borderline capable of washing hair, but cutting is a no-no."

He looked crestfallen. "Just one little experiment?" he coaxed. "Wouldn't you like to try the wedge? It's all the rage with the new wave rock stars."

"Where's Nancy?" She was getting desperate imagining what her hair would look like once Michael put his theories into action.

Luckily Nancy was coming back into the shop at that very moment. In her arms was a tray with a cake covered with candles. She smiled at Shelley, hid the cake, and motioned toward Michael to keep her occupied.

"I'm getting a bad feeling about this," Shelley

said, her voice low with a foreboding of doom. "Just what have you set in motion here?"

"I like birthday parties, don't you?" he asked pleasantly. He went back to drying her hair with the towel. "They're such cheery affairs. Everyone gets to eat cake and feel good . . ."

"It's not my birthday, Michael."

"Isn't it? How was I to know?"

"It was a pretty good guess. One chance out of three hundred and sixty-five that you might be wrong."

"Odds like that just challenge me." He grinned, putting down the towel. "It was the only way I could think of to get her to leave you alone so that I could get to you. I slipped her some loose change to go next door to the bakery. Told her it was a surprise for your birthday."

"Michael!"

But it was too late. The candles had been lit. All the staff and half the patrons were advancing on her, Nancy and the cake in the lead. The strains of "Happy Birthday to You" were beginning to lilt through the air. Shelley sat and watched them come, nonplussed. There was no way she could tell these good people the truth at this stage. She looked at the smiles on their faces. Michael was right. Birthday parties were cheery affairs. They were feeling good. And what did it hurt?

"I'll see you soon, Shelley." He leaned down near her face, then just grazed her cheek with a quick kiss. "Have a nice party."

"But—" She didn't want him to go. Suddenly she knew she never wanted him to go again. She loved him, loved him so much, she knew it was hopeless to try to pretend she could stifle the emotion. She reached out toward him and he took her hand, squeezing it for just a moment.

"I've got to go," he told her. "I just wanted to

make sure you didn't forget me." And then he was disappearing through the advancing celebrators.

Forget him. Was he crazy? She would never forget him as long as she lived, even if she never saw him again. But she had to see him again. And she knew she would. She laughed and ate cake and had her hair cut, but he was never out of her mind for a moment. She loved him so much. What was she going to do about it?

Carrie was bouncing off the walls when Shelley got home from work that night. Shelley tried to figure out what was going on, but all she could get out of Carrie were unintelligible squeaks and squeals, with a lot of waving about of paper things. Finally she grabbed away one of the papers and read it. It was a letter from Jim.

"A round-trip ticket." Carrie was finally able to form real words. "A round-trip ticket. I'm turning it in."

Joy was blooming all over the woman, and she was talking about turning in a round-trip ticket to Rio de Janeiro? Shelley was thoroughly confused, so she tried to read the letter.

"He wants you to meet him in Rio to talk things over," she said, looking puzzled.

"Yes!" Carrie squealed. "And he doesn't even know about the letter I sent him, where I absolutely groveled at his feet. Oh, he's so wonderful, I'm so lucky, how could I ever have let him out of my sight?" She grabbed away the letter and kissed it soundly.

Shelley shook her head. "But you're turning the ticket in? I don't get it."

"Of course, silly. He sent a round-trip ticket so I could come back if I want to. But I don't want to! I'm going to turn it in for a one-way. Do you think that will convince him I mean it?"

Shelley grinned. "It convinces me."

The evening was filled with furious packing and lots of hugging and not a few tears. In the morning Carrie was off to the airport, and Shelley was left to worry about her own romance once again.

Ten

Shelley always wore her glasses when she lectured at the local college as part of the adult-education extension program. She wore her hair back in what she thought of as a sophisticated twist, dressed in suits, and tried to look as professional as she could. That was the only way she could face all those people every Thursday night.

Her class wasn't large. There were twelve participants on most nights, men and women in their late twenties to mid-thirties, serious people who wanted to find out how to gain control of their lives.

The room they used was small and intimate, carpeted and furnished with armchairs, more like an office than a classroom. The members of the class could draw their chairs up close to the desk from which she lectured. She liked to encourage class participation. She felt that the class members were getting into it more if they had to make comments and think out questions.

The class was called Getting in Touch—with You! She hadn't named it. The course had actually been offered for years, and she'd been asked to take over barely three months before when the psychologist who usually ran it took a much-needed sabbatical.

This Thursday night she'd almost called the session off. She was feeling tense and excited, sure that Michael was about to drop some sort of bombshell, and she couldn't keep her mind on her research. But responsibility took the upper hand, and she'd shown up right on time. She worked on papers while the people filtered in, so it wasn't until the bell rang and she rose to lean against the front of the desk and begin her lecture that she saw the new member at the back of the class.

Everyone else faded from her consciousness as she checked him out. The white polo shirt and dark slacks were fine, but the hair was parted in the middle and slicked down, and he wore round, owl-eyed glasses. There was a notebook on his knee and a pen in his hand. He was obviously ready and eager for information. He looked as though his name should be Horatio, Shelley thought. But it wasn't. It was Michael.

She looked away quickly, before he could glance up and catch her eye. She had to take a moment to control the bubble of laughter that was trying to escape up her throat. Coughing, she adjusted her glasses and raised her head again.

"Excuse me," she said in a strained voice. "May I ask what you're doing here?"

All the others in the room turned to look at Michael, and he smiled at them, his face open and angelic. "I'm Mike Daniels," he said with happy innocence. "I'm just auditing."

"Just . . . auditing?" She noticed quite a glow

centered just about over her heart. She was glad he was here. "Fine," she told him. "You just go ahead and audit. And if you have any questions, don't hesitate to ask." She smiled at him. He smiled back, but it was Mike Daniels, not Michael Harper. She turned back to the class.

"Last week we started looking at games and how we all play them," she began. "We talked about how games are transactions we set up to protect ourselves. We talked about how we try to cover up our weaknesses with them, how they keep us apart from those we love and want to get closer to. I asked you to chart a twenty-four-hour period, trying to pinpoint the different games you found yourself playing. Did you all do that?" Heads nodded, smiles popped out. "Good. Who would like to share their findings with the rest of us?"

She went on just as she did every Thursday night, only this time everything seemed heightened. There was a tension in the room, and it stemmed right from Michael's eyes. It was exciting, but she began to wonder when he would do something outrageous. As time passed and he sat quietly, as though he really were only auditing, she realized with a start that she was disappointed.

Was she going nuts? Did she really like it when he did crazy things?

Yes, something deep inside cried out. *I love it.*

So when she saw his hand shoot up at the back of the room, she turned to him almost eagerly. "Mr. Daniels?" she asked, heart beating a little more quickly.

"Ms. Pride." He stood beside his chair to address her, though it wasn't the custom in the class. "I can't help but think there's something missing here."

He looked so goofy in the round glasses, she found herself grinning in spite of what he said. "What's that?"

"Well, you call your class Getting in Touch—with You. But I don't see much touching going on." He waved toward the others. "No physical contact whatsoever."

Uh-oh. Maybe she'd been a bit rash to wish for this. "You see, Mr. Daniels, by getting in touch, we mean in the emotional sense."

He shook his head, obviously unsatisfied. "Look, I just moved to California and I want to get involved in that stuff you always hear goes on out here. Why, you're famous for it! You know what I mean." He glanced significantly at the others. "Some of that touchie-feelie therapy."

Oh, brother. Michael, don't do this to me! "Mr. Daniels—"

He looked at the others as though he thought they might back him up. "I mean, I thought we'd switch off the lights, slip out of our clothes and pour out a little Mazola oil. Didn't you?"

There were a few snickers in the class, but he hadn't won them over. Not yet. "Mr. Daniels, if you'll just wait and talk to me about this after class . . ."

"I mean, you know?" He went on as though she hadn't spoken. "We've got better stuff than this back home. I've been really getting into it, and it's helped me a lot." He gestured, palms open. "Maybe the rest of you would like to hear about some of the things we do there."

Shelley's quick survey of the room showed that they would indeed like to hear about them. The grins were proof of that. Everyone in front of Michael turned in their seats, afraid they might miss something if they weren't careful.

"Ms. Pride?" Was he actually asking her permission? How noble of him, she thought.

"I'm sure we'd all enjoy hearing some of your experiences," she said weakly. There really wasn't much choice.

"Right." He gave her a jaunty grin. "The best thing we've got going is a little something I like to call the Julie Daniels method of self-realization."

Shelley held her breath, dark eyes wide. God only knew what he was up to.

"I learned it from a lovely psychologist," he went on blithely, eyes narrowing as he looked at her, "whose neck I'd like to bite right now," he added softly, then hurried on. "The way it works is, everyone lies down on the floor and puts his head on the next person's tummy."

Everyone in his audience looked stunned, but intrigued. Luckily they hadn't seemed to notice his mention of biting necks. Shelley flushed, but they weren't watching her.

"Here you go." He offered his hand to Mrs. Prockter, helping her to the carpeted floor. "You first. Then you"—he pointed to the man next to her—"put your head on her stomach. Then you"—he pointed to Janie Freed—"put your head on his. . . ."

They were doing it. Shelley watched, mouth hanging open, as each of her students gladly followed Michael's insane instructions. No one made a murmur of protest. Didn't they know this was ridiculous? Soon there was a chain of people lying on the floor, each with his head on someone else's stomach. They were beginning to laugh. Shelley knew what was coming.

"Mr. Daniels," she said, her voice a little high, a little unsteady, "this isn't valid therapy. This is like a children's slumber party!"

His smile was wide and knowing. "Ain't that the way? Doesn't everything ultimately stem from our childhood? So if we can just go back and recapture that youth, how lucky we will be."

The laughter was ringing through the room. As each person laughed he bounced his partner's head, making him laugh, and so on, until everyone was doing it. Shelley didn't know whether to laugh herself or cry.

"Michael," she pleaded. "This is chaos!"

He winked. "Your freckles are dancing again," he told her. "Just you wait. This is going to get better."

"Oh, no. What are you planning?"

"Our escape." He bobbed his eyebrows at her. "Leave it to me." He turned back to the class. "Just a moment, everyone."

They raised their heads, holding back the laughter.

"No, don't get up. Continue with what you're doing. I'm just going to give you a little demonstration of an advanced form of this self-realization exercise. I advise taking this step only after serious preparation. And it may not be for everyone. But Ms. Pride has agreed to help me demonstrate it for those who are interested."

Ms. Pride had done nothing of the sort, but she found herself involved nonetheless. There was a buzzing in her ears as Michael turned toward her. When he took off his glasses, laying them on the desk, then reached for hers, she put up no resistance. It seemed almost as though he were moving in slow motion.

"Put your hands out like this," he told her, and his voice sounded as though it were coming from far away.

She put out her hands to the side of her shoulders, elbows bent, just as he was showing her, and he touched her palms with his own.

"Close your eyes and breathe deeply—one, two, three times." His voice was soothing, like the sound of a brook flowing past a sunny picnic spot. She closed her eyes and listened to it, breathing as he'd told her to.

"Keep breathing." He was closer now. She could hear him, feel his breath on her cheek. "Keep breathing." When his lips touched hers, she wasn't startled. She'd been expecting it. His mouth was warm and tender, moving against hers with sweet affection, and she sighed, her eyes still closed.

His lips slid across hers and his tongue came out, prying gently, coaxing her lips to part. She opened to him slowly, almost as though she were hypnotized. And then he was inside, his tongue hot with the emotions that coursed in his veins. She heard a low sound in his throat, a sort of purr of passion, meant only for her, and she felt her body begin to respond, heating slowly, as though hot liquid were pouring down, first through her chest, then filling her abdomen, then down slowly, oh so slowly, through her thighs. She was quivering. Could he feel it? Of course he could. He could feel everything.

His palms still faced hers, holding steady. But he moved his body closer so that his wide chest just grazed the tips of her breasts, and she gasped at the sensation that shot through her at the touch.

She tried to open her eyes, but the way the room was spinning, she quickly closed them again, sighing, "Oh, Michael," and swaying against him. All control was gone and she didn't care who knew it. Suddenly she felt his hands leave hers, then he was scooping her up, one arm under her knees, the other behind her neck. Instead of fighting it, she snuggled against his chest, eyes still closed.

Had she died without noticing? This certainly felt like heaven. Here she was a serious professional woman with responsibilities, and she was going to forget all about them. But she refused to feel guilty. She wanted to be with Michael more than anything in the world. If he would have her, she was ready. Anything, anywhere; it was his decision. She loved him so much, she couldn't do anything else.

So she lay back in his arms, her soft leather

pumps dangling from her big toes, and rubbed up against him like a fluffy cat, purring her contentment. To hell with the rest of the world.

"Ms. Pride has fainted," Michael was announcing to the amused class, which was buzzing with astonishment. "That's one of the side effects of this treatment that you have to beware of. Which is why I recommend you try it only after further counseling." He bent his head to bury his face in her hair for a moment, and when he came up again, his voice was thick and husky. "I'm going to have to administer first aid, I'm afraid. She'll need a full treatment."

"Where—where are you taking her?" one of the students asked in a quavery voice as Michael started toward the door, still carrying her.

"I've got a great little first aid kit at home," he reassured them, continuing to the doorway. "Don't worry. I've dealt with cases like this before." He paused, looking back. "Will one of you please take care of her books? Take them to the office. And tell them she won't be back tonight. Thanks a lot."

Shelley finally opened her eyes as they went out the door. The members of the class were still strewn out across the floor, though most of them were sitting up. And everyone was watching them leave. Reactions varied from outright mirth to frowning disbelief. She looked up groggily at Michael's handsome face.

"They're not doing anything," she complained sleepily. "You'd think they could at least have the decency to call the police."

He chuckled. "Now what would they want to do that for?"

"I'm being kidnapped before their eyes, that's what for. Don't you think that's worth a quick call to the local law?"

"Not a chance." He pressed the button for the elevator, kissing her softly at the same time. "They know a love affair made in heaven when they see one."

He carried her almost all the way home. If he could have figured out a way to fit her under the steering wheel, she was convinced he'd probably have carried her in the car, too, right on his lap. She insisted she could walk when they arrived at his apartment building, but he wouldn't hear of it.

"It's just an illusion of well-being," he informed her. "Happens every time. You can't be trusted."

"What do you think I'm going to do, run off down the street?"

But he wouldn't budge. So he lifted her and carried her through his parking lot to another elevator. She didn't complain very vigorously. His shoulders were so wide and comforting, and he smelled so good. She just lay back and enjoyed it.

"Here we are." He kicked open the door to his apartment and carried her across the threshold.

"You should save that for your bride," she chided him softly.

"What do you think you are?" he responded, still holding her.

She stiffened against him. What was he talking about? Was he joking? If so, it would be best to get it out in the open right now. "You once said not to expect any white lace," she reminded him, trying to keep up the illusion that she was taking all this as lightheartedly as he seemed to be.

"So, wear pink lace," he grumbled. "Or better yet, don't wear anything at all." His warm lips were just in front of her ear, dropping a soft kiss. "Don't bother me with details. I'm too busy loving you." He kissed her again. "I want to love you all over."

"Michael . . ." She struggled to sit upright in his arms.

He sighed. "Going too fast, huh? You like a little

more finesse in the approach, I suppose? All right." He dropped her unceremoniously on the couch. "Would you like a drink, madam?" he asked formally. "A nice little meal? We can always have some roast chicken brought in. A soothing bath?" He raised an eyebrow at the idea, then grinned. "We aim to please."

She laughed up at him. "A drink, please," she said, mostly to give her something to do with her hands and a shield to hide behind while she got her bearings. "Something light and cool."

She looked around the apartment while he left the room to make the drinks. It was surprisingly sterile, simple, and standard, with none of the personal touches she would have expected from a man with his vibrant personality. But then she remembered. He never stayed in one place long enough to put down roots. All of this anonymous-looking furniture was most likely rented by the month. She felt suddenly cold.

Her glance caught on something out of place. There was a photograph in a gold frame on the desk along the far wall. He couldn't have rented that, could he? Maybe it would give her a clue to his life. She rose and went to it. It was a picture of her.

"Where did you get this?" she asked Michael as he came back into the room, two tall drinks in his hands.

He came up behind her and smiled. "That picture has kept me warm on more than one long, lonely night. Cute, isn't she?"

"I don't know." She picked up the photo and held it out, examining it critically. "A little bouncy-looking for my taste."

"You think so?" He frowned at the picture, pretending to consider her opinion. "You may be right. Sort of cocker spaniel puppy, wouldn't you say?"

She met his gaze and laughed. "Thanks a lot." Putting down the picture, she turned back to him. "But where did you get it?"

"Carrie gave it to me the night I appeared in your apartment looking like something left over from a fifties motorcycle movie. She took pity on me, I guess."

Shelley remembered the picture. Carrie had taken it when they'd spent an afternoon in the San Gabriel Mountains a few months before. She wondered why Carrie hadn't told her she'd given Michael a copy. It looked like her roomie was doing a little matchmaking on the side, no matter how much she professed to be a supporter of Shelley's failed plan.

Michael steered her toward the couch and sat her down. "So much for the small talk," he announced. With one swift movement he pulled the pins from her hair and she shook it out so that it flew around her head like a bright golden halo. "Now I'm going to ply you with liquor. Drink up."

She grinned, looking up at him. "Ply away," she told him, "but it's not going to do you a whole lot of good if you don't do something about your own hair. Really, Michael, you look so silly. Do you always go overboard on your disguises?"

He pulled a comb out of his pocket and set his hair to rights. "This isn't a disguise," he told her haughtily. "It's called getting a feel for the character."

She smiled. "You're a character, all right," she teased, then a frown crept over her face. "But who's the real Michael Harper?" she asked softly.

He didn't seem to sense the unease behind her words. Spreading out his hands, he said, "What you see is what you get."

Shelley made a sudden resolution. "Sit," she told him, pointing to the far end of the couch while she settled herself in the opposite corner, facing where she wanted him to put himself. "You're going to tell me all about yourself."

"You want me to sit all the way down there?" he complained. "I'll have to shout to make myself heard."

"Then shout," she told him firmly. "I want to hear your whole history with no distractions." After all, who was this man she loved? She knew almost nothing about him. What had made him opt for this crazy life he led? She had to begin to gather clues, at least.

He hesitated, then did as she'd ordered, looking grumpy. "You want to analyze me, right?" he accused. "You want to pick me apart, identify my yin and yang, pin me to the wall like a butterfly."

"Why not?" Shelley was beginning to enjoy this. She laced her fingers together on her lap. "You intrigue me."

He sniffed. "Okay, here goes. I was born in a little town in Louisiana. My parents were nice to me. No interesting traumas that come readily to mind. I went to school, dated pretty girls, went away to college, got a job, and here I am."

She groaned, exasperated. "Short and sweet, but hardly revealing."

"Revealing." He grinned and stretched out to cover his end of the couch. "You want revealing?" Reaching out, he took hold of one soft leather pump and pulled it from her foot. "I'll show you revealing."

He pulled off her other shoe before she had a chance to draw back her leg, then dropped both shoes on the floor beside the couch.

"Michael, come on." She wiggled her toes at him, not really upset. "Tell me something that will let me know why you are the way you are."

His large hand covered her foot and began massaging gently. "Why don't you let me tell you in body language?" he asked. "I'm much more articulate that way."

His touch tickled through her nylons, but it still felt heavenly. "Someone stole your bike when you were thirteen," she guessed out of the blue. "You were so outraged, you vowed to spend the rest of your life fighting crime."

His laugh was loud and open. "Nope. Good try though."

She sat up higher and he followed her, coming closer across the couch, his hand on her calf.

"Your father was a prosecuting attorney who imbued you with the love of the law."

He shook his head. "My dad was a farmer," he said simply. "I still own the farm. My Aunt Marta lives there and watches over it for me."

"Your Aunt Marta?" It sounded so homey.

"Yeah, you're going to like her. She'll tell you everything you want to know, from what color pajamas I wore right on up to the mistakes in grammar I make in my letters to her right now. Just wait. You'll be meeting her soon." His hand was making lazy circles on her flesh.

He was making it all sound as though he were really serious about getting married. But if he really was, why hadn't he asked her? He treated everything as a joke. It was pretty tough getting a fix on what he really meant, and what he thought would make a good laugh.

"Did you hate farming? Was that the motivation to leave?"

He grinned, his hand moving higher, rubbing gently on the inner plane of her thigh. "I love farming. I'm going to go back to the old place someday. You're going to like it. It's got a big old Colonial-type house on it, stables and all that stuff. Someday we'll fix it up like it should be."

We, he said. Her heart was beating faster. He was

sounding an awful lot like a man who meant business. "So why did you leave?"

"I wanted to be an actor."

That surprised her. "An actor?"

He nodded. "I went to New York. Spent some time in summer stock. Tried Hollywood. Even had a part in a television series that ran for two years. But something was missing. I hated standing around learning lines other people wrote." His smile was self-deprecatory. "I was always sure I could have written a better script myself. But the whole thing was too boring." He was very close now, and suddenly his hand was under her skirt, peeling away her panty hose. That startled her, but his touch seemed so benign. Anyway, she was too interested in what he had to say to want to stop him now.

"Then I gave it all up and went to law school."

"That must have been boring too," she commented, watching almost abstractedly as he removed her hose and threw them on the coffee table.

He shook his head. "I was studying too hard to be bored. But later, when I joined a law firm, that was boring."

His hand was on her thigh again, and little shivers of excitement were sparking from his touch.

"So when I got a chance to do undercover work, I jumped at it. I get to act, but I make up my own lines."

There it was again. He went where the action was. The feeling of dread was there in the pit of her stomach again. How long would he be happy with a stay-at-home like her?

No, she wasn't going to think about that. She was here because she loved him. She wanted to be with him for as long as she could, whatever that took. She wanted to lie by his side, to feel his blood quicken as she touched him, to take him to her and carry him beyond thought, into that magic place where the air exploded and fire lit the night.

So she didn't protest as he came beside her, kissing his way up from her shoulder, nuzzling into the curve of her neck. Instead, she reached out and ran her fingers through his thick hair, gripping gently and pulling him closer.

"You are so delicious," he breathed against her skin, exploring the sensitive area behind her ear. "You're almost good enough to eat."

"Restrain yourself," she replied lightly, closing her eyes.

His arms tightened and he rubbed his face into her neck. "And you said we were incompatible," he purred.

"We are," she breathed, closing her eyes and moving aside her hair to give him more room for seductive designs on her neck.

"Like hell we are." He raised his head and looked at her. "You know what? You're a good actor. You'd make a great agent too."

She laughed softly, stretching beside him. "I'm sure I would. Can't you just see me out there, catching crooks?"

He looked almost serious. "Why not? It involves very little physical danger, you know. Most of the time anyway. You enjoyed fooling the Weekses, didn't you? And good old Harry?"

She had to admit she had, but she'd been working under Michael's guidance. She couldn't imagine doing that sort of thing for real. The idea made her giggle.

"I did like it though," she said musingly. "It was scary, but fun."

"Sure it was. You could be good at it if I let you."

"Let me?" She poked him in the ribs. "Who says you'll ever have that kind of say?"

"I do," he replied with no hesitation. "Be still, woman, and let me ravish you."

"I'm afraid I've never been much of an adventurer," she said, reaching out to push his hair back off his forehead. How she loved his bright blue eyes—they seemed to see everything, know everything, and still be curious for more. "Do you really think I could learn?"

"All you need are sleuth lessons," he said, eyes narrowing as he came close to nibble on her earlobe. "I'll teach you all the undercover operating techniques you'll ever need to know."

"Hmm." She sighed, running her hand across the rounded swell of his chest muscles.

"When I get through with you," he murmured teasingly against her parted lips. "you'll live for danger, just like I do."

She smiled and he kissed her, kissed her long and hard and gloriously, until she felt as though the walls were melting and the furniture were crumbling away to dust beneath them; as though a Wagnerian opera were taking place in her head and some fine Flamenco dancing were going on in her heart.

"Oh, Michael," she gasped when he drew away, "I don't want to live for danger. I want to live for kisses like that."

"That was just your first lesson, pilgrim. Undercover affairs are very complex, but you're a quick study, I can tell."

His hands slid beneath the lapels of her suit jacket and then he was tugging it off. "The next lesson involves quick change," he said. "A good agent knows how to move from one identity to another in the time it takes to switch hats." He began to work on the buttons of her silk blouse with careful determination.

"Kind of like Clark Kent in the phone booth?" she asked.

"Exactly." Her blouse came off even more easily than the jacket, and she reached to pull his shirt out of its tuck into his slacks. "You never know when you'll need to make a fast getaway as anonymously as possible."

She nodded groggily, reaching beneath the cloth to capture his warmth in the palm of her hand. He smiled and shrugged off the shirt, giving her free rein to explore his chest.

"An agent should know how to be seductive," he whispered, taking her face between his hands and gazing down at her. "How to entice the suspect just so far and no farther."

"Show me," she whispered back, and he guided her with his hands until she'd arched toward him just enough to let him unclasp her bra and slip it off. Her breasts seemed to swell against his warm chest, nipples tangling in the curling chest hair, and she moaned, feeling her hips began to move of their own volition.

"Uh-uh," he warned teasingly, stopping her with his hand. "You've got to learn to hide your reactions, to keep your emotions under wraps. Invincible bravery under fire. A stony exterior in the face of the enemy." He grinned. "Never let on how good this feels."

"I'll try not to," she whispered against incredible odds. "I'll be brave. I promise."

He pressed her back against the couch and began to explore her neck, her collar bone, the soft, smooth slope of her breast, with lips and tongue, licking, nipping, kissing, until she thought she would go mad with longing for him.

"Don't move," he reminded her as his teeth closed on one nipple, tugging gently while his tongue caressed the very tip. His hand slipped beneath the band of her skirt, reaching under the silky nylon.

"Michael," she gasped, no longer able to hold back. "Oh Michael, I need you so!"

His answer was more a low, animal growl than a

word, and suddenly she found herself swept up in his arms once again. She closed her eyes, opening them when he put her on his bed. All she could see was the blue of his eyes, all she could feel was an overwhelming hunger that only he could fulfill.

She reached for his belt buckle while he unbuttoned her skirt, and in another moment they were both naked and clinging together as though nothing would ever be able to part them. The ache, the need to be closer, closer, was so real, she cried out with it, digging her fingers into his back and he responded, his hard, smooth body made only for her. Together they climbed as high as they dared, together they gloried in the incredible joy they found there, and together they slid back down again, landing in a thump among the rumpled covers.

For a long moment they lay there, so tightly wound together, they might have been one. Shelley listened to his heart beat slow, just as her own was. She loved him so dearly. How could she ever let him go?

Michael was the one who spoke first. "So it was true," he said huskily.

"Hmm?" she asked, letting her head fall back on the pillow.

He kissed her neck. "That first time we made love. I thought maybe I'd imagined how good it was. I was worried about that."

She chuckled, reaching to smooth back his hair. "You could have asked me," she told him softly. "I would've told you."

"Tell me now," he murmured. "Whisper sweet nothings in my ear. And then tell me you'll marry me on Sunday."

She raised up on her elbow. "Why Sunday?" she asked, sure there was still a joke lurking in there somewhere.

He stretched his magnificent body beside her.

"Because by Sunday, I should be finished with the case I'm working on right now. And that will be my last undercover case with the department."

Conflicting reactions rushed through her mind. "What do you mean? Are you leaving?"

"No." He reached up and began to trace the features of her face with his index finger. "But I'm getting out of undercover work for a while." He grinned. "I've got something more exciting in mind."

Still totally at sea, anxiety was growing inside her. "What?"

"Getting married." He tapped the end of her nose. "Starting a family. Making a real life for us." His hand cupped her chin. "What do you say, lady shrink? Will you marry me?"

Would she? Would she put on rags and go begging in the street for him? Would she climb Mt. Everest if he asked her to? Anything. Everything. He had only to say the word. But she still was shaky about this. She hadn't expected him to be so serious. "What will you do?"

He smiled. "There are lots of other slots I can fill at the district attorney's office. My first choice would be director of undercover work, supervising the sort of operations I know so well. But there are plenty of other interesting jobs for a trained lawyer. I'll be busy for some time prosecuting the cases I've been working on here. I'd like to stick with them right through conviction and sentencing. Then I'll be looking into other options." He touched her softly. "Don't worry about me. I'll keep busy."

Was he doing all this for her? She couldn't believe it. "But will you be able to keep from getting bored?" she asked earnestly.

"That will be your job," he told her, grinning, then his face changed and his voice was serious. "Don't worry about that. I told you the thrills haven't been what they once were. That was why

I'd started doing stupid things to liven them up. I think I've reached the saturation point. I'm burned out and ready for a change."

He took her hair in his hand. "You know, I think I knew the minute I saw you standing there in the department store that you were going to be special in my life." His eyes crinkled at the corners. "I think I loved you from the very first time you had me arrested. That'll be something to tell our kids, won't it?"

She laughed. It was really happening. They were going to get married. All her doubts, all her fears, were evaporating around her, and something very rich and warm was growing in her chest.

"I knew I'd better stay away from you," he went on. "It was a real temptation to drop in on you that day I had the first appointment with Jerry Kramer."

"You left your matches in the ashtray," she reminded him. "Did you do that on purpose?"

His chuckle rocked the bed. "I don't know. You're the psychologist. Probably so. I know I stood around lighting that cigarette for an awfully long time, hoping you would come out of your office."

Her eyes opened wide. "I haven't ever seen you have a cigarette since," she said.

He shrugged. "I don't smoke." His dancing eyes met hers. "I borrowed it from your secretary."

Then, like little kids, they were giggling and rolling across the bed. "Anyway," he went on once he'd wrestled her back under control, "when you fell into my lap in Newport, I knew I was in real trouble. There was no way I could resist your aggressive advances."

"What?"

"Sure." He looked so innocent. "You practically attacked me in front of the whole world. I had to draft you into playing my wife to save you from embarrassment."

That earned him a pillow to the head, but it didn't stop the flow of his reminiscences. "But I still fought it. I thought maybe we could have a fling and then I'd move on, like I've always done in the past. I soon learned my mistake. When you tried to tell me to get lost, I knew there was no way I could ever leave you behind." He bent down and kissed her, and she smiled and snuggled against him.

"What do you have left to do on this last case?" she asked, playing with the hair on his chest, whirling it around her finger.

"I'm meeting with a consortium at a party on a yacht, back down in Newport. These people will think I'm a wealthy sucker from New Jersey. They'll try to sell me on buying a yacht that can be used in a complicated lease-back scheme. I'll get the goods on them, we'll get them arrested, and I'll be ready for Sunday." He kissed her ear. "Will you be?"

She wiggled her toes. "I want to go too." And suddenly, it was true. She realized that she really did.

"What?" He looked wary. "Where?"

"I want to go to the party on the yacht." She went on quickly when she could see *no* forming in his eyes. "You said yourself that I wasn't too bad with the Weekses and with Harry." She bounced up to sit beside him. "And I wasn't, was I? It was fun. And I want to do it again."

"This one will be a little more dangerous . . ." he began, but she wouldn't give him a chance to finish.

"After all these good undercover techniques you've been teaching me, how can I fail?" She kissed him on the temple. "Really, Michael. I'll be careful. I won't goof anything up for you." She grinned. "It'll be fun."

"I can see it now," he groaned. "I no sooner get

out of the business than my shy little wife gets into it."

"No." She shook her head. "I'm going to be too busy learning what married life is all about to do that. But—just this once. What do you say?"

He pulled her down on top of him. "I can't say no to you," he said huskily. "Not ever."

"I'll need a gown to wear to the party," she said musingly. "I know exactly where to get one too."

He was on her wavelength. "The one you were trying on at the department store?"

"Right." She sat up. "And I'll need some jewelry to go with it. . . ." Her eyes were sparkling.

He groaned. "You've been bitten by the bug, that's obvious." Pulling her back down again, he tousled her hair. "What a life we'll have together. We'll spend most of the year with our noses to our respective grindstones, then we'll take our vacations in exotic places and hire out as amateur detectives, like that couple on television."

She was too full of excitement to stay in one place for more than ten seconds at a time, and she bounced back up again. "Could we? That sounds great. We could start in Peru and visit Carrie and Jim. I'll make reservations on Monday morning. . . ."

He tackled her before she could fly away, and this time he pinned her down with his long body. "Hey, listen. I can't tell if you're more interested in marrying me or adopting my life-style."

Her dark eyes misted over. She raised her hand and touched his cheek. "I love you, undercover man," she said with husky sincerity. "I've loved you forever, and I'll go on loving you forevermore."

He kissed the end of her nose, then couldn't resist her lips. "You wouldn't con me, would you, woman?" he whispered, beginning to move against her.

She didn't have to answer. Not with words. Her

brimming eyes, and the immediate response of her body, were all the reply he needed.

THE EDITOR'S CORNER

Please be sure to turn to the back of this book for a special treat—an excerpt from the novel **CHASE THE MOON** by a marvelous British author, Catherine Nicolson. I hope the short sample of this extraordinarily romantic story will prompt you to ask your bookseller for the book next month when you get your four LOVESWEPTs. And, of course, we believe those four LOVESWEPTs are real treats, too!

It astonishes me at times how our authors continue to top themselves book after book. They're all talented authors who are devoted to expanding their imaginations and developing the skills of their craft. And I know how hard they work. Still, I'm often surprised at the high level of creativity they are able to maintain. And no author demonstrates better those qualities of originality and ingenuity in superb romantic storytelling than Kay Hooper.

IF THERE BE DRAGONS, LOVESWEPT #71, is one of Kay's most emotionally touching romances. The surprises you expect from a Kay Hooper book are abundant in this story of lovely Brooke Kennedy whose rare gift has kept her a virtual prisoner of loneliness. But, thanks to that delightful meddler Pepper, a golden knight comes to her rescue. Cody Nash, Thor's best friend in **PEPPER'S WAY,** enters Brooke's world and brings her the warmth and light of love. I'll never forget Brooke and her dragons, Cody and his virile tenderness . . . or a very special "wild" creature who contributes a unique and heartwarming dimension to this wonderful story.

(continued)

Sandra Kleinschmit makes her debut as a published author next month with a nifty romance, **PROBABLE CAUSE**, LOVESWEPT #72. Jami Simpson isn't playing cops and robbers when she detains a man she suspects of breaking and entering. She's a police officer all right, but Lance Morgan is hardly a burglar . . . or is he? He assaults Jami's emotions and tries to steal her heart in a love story that's sensitive and fun. We hope you'll join us in giving this brand new author the warmly enthusiastic welcome you've given the other talented writers we've been so pleased to be able to publish for the first time.

And speaking of new talents, here comes BJ James again with **MORE THAN FRIENDS**, LOVESWEPT #73. BJ's first book, **WHEN YOU SPEAK LOVE**, was vibrant with dramatic tension, though touched with humor; her second romance shows her versatility in a work that's full of charming lightheartedness, though touched with dramatic tension. The heroine of **MORE THAN FRIENDS** is pocket-sized Jamie, the sister of six brawny males. She's grown up in a household devoted to competitive sports and has always been in the thick of rough and tumble football games and fierce races, never asking for privilege because of her sex or size. Then she literally tackles a gentle giant named Mike Bradford and he tries to turn her life around. You'll be as appalled—and impressed—as Mike is by Jamie's foolish physical courage . . . and her confusion about the conflict between competition and independence. What a love story!

Ah, it is such a delight for me to tell you about **CHARADE**, LOVESWEPT #74, by Joan Elliott Pickart. This sensual love story is spiked by some of the most amusing exchanges it's been my pleasure to read. (One line in particular struck me as so side-splittingly funny that my son ran into the room where I was reading to see if I was choking!) **CHARADE,** as the title suggests, is a merry romance in which heroine Whitney assumes a false identity . . . and gets trapped (hmm, quite deliciously) in her role by one of the most captivating of all possible heroes. The marvelous cast of secondary characters—from a soap opera heart-throb to a babbling would-be vamp—truly enrich this tale. Watch out for the hero's dear old gray-haired Aunt Olive. She has a surprise or two up her sleeve!

Enjoy! And do continue to write to us. Your comments are so helpful and so interesting!

Warm good wishes,
Sincerely,

Carolyn Nichols

Carolyn Nichols
  Editor
LOVESWEPT
Bantam Books, Inc.
666 Fifth Avenue
New York, NY 10103

Dear LOVESWEPT reader:

CHASE THE MOON is a one-in-a-million book, the kind of story that won't let you rest until you've finished it, and then won't fade from your heart and mind for months. Set apart from other novels in the romance genre by its un- usual blend of the richly exotic and the touch- ingly innocent, CHASE THE MOON is a fairy tale for grown-ups, created of mystery and magic, beauty and sensuality, fantasy and fulfillment. And next month it will be available from your bookseller.

The heroine's name is Corrie Modena, alias Columbine. A naive, lonely orphan whose stun- ning musical talent drives her in search of fame and fortune, she has confided her secret dreams to only one man—an enigmatic stranger she knows only through letters signed Harlequin. Al- though they have never met, theirs is a perfect, trusting love . . . until the night that Corrie meets Guy de Chardonnet at the opera. The magnetic attraction that Corrie and Guy feel is immediate and fierce, although they are constantly at odds with each other. But Corrie is torn between Guy and her burning ambition, an ambition that Harlequin, in his letters, urges her not to betray. Corrie determines to leave Guy, realizing that Harlequin is right—for how can she know that the man to whom she's lost her heart is the steadfast keeper of her soul?

The storyline is magical, but what makes CHASE THE MOON truly unique is the extraordinary way in which the story is told. The writing is exquisitely sensual, skillfully evoking the sights, smells, tactile experiences, tastes, and sounds of the world Corrie and Guy share—a world of light: an apricot moon hanging in the still azure sky above the Riviera; sunlight; stage lighting; the dazzling spangles and sequins refracting light on costumes; the play of shadow and moonlight spilling into the nighttime ocean. Even Corrie's voice is described as having the deep and dark quality of "L'heure bleue," the strange blue hour between summer twilight and summer night. Dusky, fragrant, and everchanging, the world of CHASE THE MOON is memorable and magical, even to its elusive characters: the "real" Guy and Corrie, the fantasy Harlequin and Columbine. And CHASE THE MOON could perhaps only have been written by Catherine Nicolson—a lovely woman from Great Britain who possesses abundant charm and talent.

CHASE THE MOON is spellbinding . . . a world of romantic fantasies come breathtakingly true— where two lovers have no secrets from each other . . . except their names. It was a special delight for me to be Catherine's editor on this book. I hope the excerpt on the following pages will captivate you so much that you'll be sure to ask your bookseller for CHASE THE MOON.

Carolyn Nichols

Chase the Moon

by Catherine Nicolson

He had invited her to Paradise to enjoy oysters and peacocks . . . and she'd been unable to resist.

She turned, slowly. He looked different, younger. Against the white of his suit his skin was lightly tanned, with a satiny evenness that disturbed her. His hair, touched by the late sun, had reddish hints. Only his ice-gray eyes were unchanged. She felt suddenly confused. Perhaps in these few short weeks he had grown younger and she had grown older, perhaps they were growing together, like herself and the Balenciaga . . . She halted the thought. It didn't make sense.

"You don't seem surprised." She spoke abruptly to hide her confusion.

"Should I be?" He smiled at her, a lazy, self-assured, mocking smile.

"I might not have come."

His smile deepened, touched his eyes briefly.

"I knew you would come. You wouldn't be able to resist it. The oysters or the peacocks would persuade you, one or the other. And curiosity. All women like the same things."

"Really?" She spoke with some asperity. She was not and would never be like all women. "What might those things be?"

He smiled down at her lazily, shrugged.

"Silk. Paris. Compliments. Surprises." He offered her his arm. "Besides . . ." His tone was gently conversational. "I always get what I want."

"Always?" She was uneasily aware of the warmth of his skin through the soft material of his sleeve.

"Almost always."

Ceremoniously he escorted her back to the table overlooking the garden. She felt strange, as if she were in a dream. The restaurant was still deserted, they had the whole gallery room to themselves. It made her feel unreal, timeless, as if they were both on a stage, acting out a kind of play for an unseen audience. A waiter materialized out of the wings. She noticed for the first time that there was no menu.

Guy nodded in response to the waiter's inquiring glance. Not a word was spoken. The waiter disappeared as silently as a fish.

"I hope you're hungry." She was conscious of his eyes on her face.

"I'm always hungry."

"I know, I remember." He smiled. She felt a blush coloring her cheeks and refused to acknowledge it. The past meant nothing, she could rise above it.

"And you . . . Are you always late?"

"Touché." He spoke mildly, offering neither explanations nor excuses. She felt a fleeting tinge of admiration. His effrontery rivaled her own, though she had to admit his had a degree more style.

The waiter reappeared, with a large tray in his arms. As he set it down carefully Corrie saw to her astonishment that it was filled from edge to edge with small shallow bowls, each containing what seemed like no more than a mouthful of different dishes. Guy dismissed the waiter with a nod of approval. Corrie stared at the table. There was scarcely a spare inch of tablecloth to be seen.

"What is this?" She looked up to find Guy studying her with that annoying hint of irony.

"You told me you wanted everything. Well, here it is. Something from every single dish on the Belvedere's not inextensive menu." Her eyes widened. "There's more to come, but there wasn't enough room on the table." His smile was limpidly ingenuous. "Eat up, or it will get cold." He handed her a small silver dish. "I suggest you begin with the smoked oysters."

The unmistakable challenge in his eyes was irresistible. Corrie instantly resolved to do justice to the feast or die in the attempt. She'd show him what it meant to be hungry.

Manfully, she set to work. He watched in growing astonishment as she polished off dish after dish, chasing the last drops of sauce with catlike delicacy. Lobster bisque and *consommé madrilène*, *chateaubriand printanier*, *suprême* of sole, artichoke hearts, soft carps' roe, lamb cutlets, veal escalopes with apples and cream, flamed in calvados, crab claws dressed in pistachio nut oil. Invisibly the empty dishes were whisked away to be replenished with tiny spring vegetables, duckling with green pepper and brandy sauce, wild strawberries, brandied peaches, chicken stuffed with braised fennel roots, shrimp soufflé . . . Recklessly she mixed sweet with savory, fish with fowl, red meat with white. It was a cornucopia of delights, a Roman orgy. White Burgundy followed red, Nuits St. Georges chasing Pouilly Fuissé, and capped with a rainbow assortment of different ice creams.

"Are you quite sure you've had enough?" His tone was elaborately solicitous as she pushed away the last ice-cream dish and patted her lips with a napkin. She nodded, so full she could barely speak.

"Yes, I think so." She glimpsed a remaining petit four and downed it with relish. "For the moment."

He shook his head in mock astonishment. "You'll be sick."

"I'm never sick. I have the digestion of a camel."

"So I see. How do you manage it?"

"It's quite simple. All you have to do is eat with your spine." She took a deep breath. "And there's something else."

"What's that?" He was regarding her with as much polite interest as he would have shown a real camel in a zoo.

"Motivation."

"Motivation?" He frowned, puzzled.

"Perhaps you've never heard of it." She allowed a slight trace of sarcasm to enter her tone. "It's called hunger."

"Indeed." He seemed unmoved, just faintly curious. "You interest me, Miss Modena. Why should a woman in your position . . ." his eyes rested lazily on her bare shoulders—"ever have to suffer such an indignity? Surely your patron cannot be such an ogre? Or is it . . ." Here his eyes took on a mocking gleam. "Can it possibly be that he prefers slender women?"

Corrie drew herself to her full height and with an heroic effort choked back her anger at the implied insult.

"M. de Chardonnet." She spoke with dignity, as befitted a widow recently bereaved. "I no longer have a patron."

"Oh." He seemed surprised, even concerned. She gritted her teeth, disguised her fury behind demurely cast down eyes. Doubtless he couldn't imagine how a young woman could survive without the support and protection of a man such as himself. "Are you no longer at the Savoy?"

"From tomorrow, no." She thought about coaxing a tear, decided against it. She was bereaved, but brave.

"Because of me?"

The effrontery of the man! He didn't seem in the least abashed—if anything he sounded pleased, almost gratified. He assumed, of course, that she'd been dismissed by her patron because of one evening spent in another man's company. Such arrogance . . .

"You could say so." She sighed deeply.

"My deepest sympathy." He was smiling a small, knowing smile, as if now at last he had her in his power.

"I don't want your sympathy, thank you very much!" A trace of tartness entered her tone. His smile broadened.

"Perhaps another petit four?"

"Certainly not." She folded her hands primly in her lap. He was still looking at her with that disturbing, assessing gaze. He gestured at the waiter to clear away the remaining dishes.

"At least you enjoyed your meal."

The touch of irony in his voice brought a blush to her cheeks. A healthy appetite hardly became the grieving widow . . . But it was too late now.

"It was delicious." Belatedly she remembered her manners. "Thank you." A thought struck her suddenly; she frowned in puzzlement. "But why has no one else come to eat here? They don't know what they're missing."

He smiled patiently.

"Because I've engaged the entire restaurant."

"What?"

Now he really had managed to surprise her. "Just for us?" It was an extraordinary extravagance, it almost made her feel ill.

"Of course."

"Do you mean . . . they've cooked all these different dishes . . . just for me?"

"Of course."

"You mean, there's a whole rack of lamb back there, and I've just had one mouthful?"

"I've no idea. I should imagine so. It hadn't occurred to me."

He smiled indulgently. "I could ask for it to be put in a bag for you, if you like. We could take it with us."

She leaned back in her chair, half amused, half appalled. He and she were worlds apart. She couldn't even begin to imagine what it must be like to live as he did, to spend as if money were a mere toy for his own amusement. And yet he himself had barely touched a mouthful of the feast.

"Why didn't you eat anything?"

He shrugged. "As you say, it is a question of . . . motivation. I preferred to watch you."

She blushed again. It hadn't been the sort of performance she'd intended. She stared at him. The light from the gardens outside was deepening infinitesimally into blue, flattering, softening, making outlines unreal.

"Now, Mademoiselle Corrie, you have done ample justice to the oysters. It is time for peacocks."

In a dream she took his proffered arm. She could no longer remember whether she liked him or not, she was too full of good food for logic. As they emerged into the air she saw there were no other people in sight. A thought struck her.

"You haven't hired the whole of the park as well?"

"No." He laughed, the deep spontaneous laugh which she was beginning to like, to try and prize out of him. Slowly they walked up toward the ornamental garden. Around them she felt the faintest stir of breeze, bringing with it the hypnotic scent of newly mown grass. Sunlight glinted off the little clocktower with its turquoise copper roof and golden ball. The old rose bricks of the arcade leading to the orangery were soft in the sunlight, the shadows violet beneath the murmuring trees. He was right. It was as near as man could get to Paradise.

Beneath the trees, in the emerald green shade where the grass bloomed with an underwater intensity, rabbits browsed while on the high old walls peacocks strutted and bowed, saluting the evening with their harsh haunting cries. Everything around them was poised timelessly on the brink of summer, every rabbit soft and fat with plenty, every peacock with its hen.

Against her will, she was drawn into the fairy-tale. She couldn't resist the peacocks. Their voices had the authority, the aching, soulful penetration of a prima donna soprano. Those slender necks and tiny heads didn't look capable of producing such a noise. And they moved so slowly, sure of their charisma, milking their audience. The last light was brilliant on their opalescent plumage. How much she wanted to be a peacock.

They halted, mesmerized. A peacock eyed them motionlessly with its malachite gaze. His snake-like neck, insufferably blue, waved, searching, swelling. He emitted a superb, spine-shaking shriek. And then slowly, like a magician, he produced his tail, spreading it like a moonscape, a heaven full of dancing planets. He stayed there, quivering for enough time to stun them, then shuffled his feathers back with a businesslike air, squawked once and stalked away.

It was a revelation. They looked at each other with a sort of awe. They had been privileged, it was as if royalty had stopped to speak to them in the street. They had shared something irreplaceable, unrepeatable.

"What was that?" Her voice was a whisper. She hardly dared to break the silence, but she wanted to spread her own plumes for him, tell him her plans and dreams, flaunt her secret inner world.

"Serendipity." He turned to her, his white suit dappled under the shimmering leaves. "I never realized . . ." His voice was soft, like someone woken from a deep sleep. "Your eyes are so blue, violet, actually."

They stared at each other. The image of the peacock's tail still seemed to be imprinted on her retina, a dazzling mist of color. She couldn't see, couldn't think.

"Come with me." His voice was low. "Come with me to Paris. Now, tonight."

Paris, Paris, Paradise . . . It sounded so easy. It would be easy. She could float away and never be heard of again, supported by him and his money, like a swimmer in the Dead Sea. But it wasn't enough, it couldn't be enough for her.

She shook her head. The peacock's plumes were fading, the moment was lost. She couldn't go to Paris with a man who'd only just noticed the color of her eyes.

Dear Harlequin,

What's happening to me? Why can't I stop thinking about him? He's nothing special, just a collection of cells and corpuscles like me, and yet I think if I saw him in the street I'd throw away everything, all the future we've planned, just to hear his voice again . . . Does that sound crazy? I wish I knew how long this was going to last. Some days I think I'm cured, I hardly think about him at all, and then at night he comes alive again as soon as I fall asleep, and I wake up crying.

I was such a fool, I don't know how I came to fall in love with him of all people. You know how I feel about rich men—surely I should have been immune?

Please, tell me I've done the right thing.

Columbine

**A Towering, Romantic Saga by the
Author of
LOVE'S WILDEST FIRES**

HEARTS
OF
FIRE

by Christina Savage

For Cassie Tryon, Independence Day, 1776, signals a
different kind of upheaval—the wild, unstoppable rebellion of her heart. For on this day, she will meet a
stranger—a legendary privateer disguised in clerk's
clothes, a mysterious man come to do secret, patriot's
business with her father . . . a man so compelling that
she knows her life will never be the same for that
meeting. He is Lucas Jericho—outlaw, rebel, avenger of
his family's fate at British hands, a man who is dangerous to love . . . and impossible to forget.

Buy HEARTS OF FIRE, on sale November 1, 1984, wherever Bantam paperbacks are sold, or use the handy
coupon below for ordering:

#1 HEAVEN'S PRICE
By Sandra Brown
Blair Simpson had enclosed herself in the fortress of her dancing, but Sean Garrett was determined to love her anyway. In his arms she came to understand the emotions behind her dancing. But could she afford the high price of love?

#2 SURRENDER
By Helen Mittermeyer
Derry had been pirated from the church by her ex-husband, from under the nose of the man she was to marry. She remembered every detail that had driven them apart—and the passion that had drawn her to him. The unresolved problems between them grew . . . but their desire swept them toward surrender.

#3 THE JOINING STONE
By Noelle Berry McCue
Anger and desire warred within her, but Tara Burns was determined not to let Damon Mallory know her feelings. When he'd walked out of their marriage, she'd been hurt.

Damon had violated a sacred trust, yet her passion for him was as breathtaking as the Grand Canyon.

#4 SILVER MIRACLES
By Fayrene Preston
Silver-haired Chase Colfax stood in the Texas moonlight, then took Trinity Ann Warrenton into his arms. Overcome by her own needs, yet determined to have him on her own terms, she struggled to keep from losing herself in his passion.

#5 MATCHING WITS
By Carla Neggers
From the moment they met, Ryan Davis tried to outmaneuver Abigail Lawrence. She'd met her match in the Back Bay businessman. And Ryan knew the Boston lawyer was more woman than any he'd ever encountered. Only if they vanquished their need to best the other could their love triumph.

#6 A LOVE FOR ALL TIME
By Dorothy Garlock
A car crash had left its marks on Casey Farrow's beauty. So what were Dan

Murdock's motives for pursuing her? Guilt? Pity? Casey had to choose. She could live with doubt and fear . . . or learn a lesson in love.

#7 A TRYST WITH MR. LINCOLN?

By Billie Green
When Jiggs O'Malley awakened in a strange hotel room, all she saw were the laughing eyes of stranger Matt Brady . . . all she heard were his teasing taunts about their "night together" . . . and all she remembered was nothing! They evaded the passions that intoxicated them until . . . there was nowhere to flee but into each other's arms.

#8 TEMPTATION'S STING

By Helen Conrad
Taylor Winfield likened Rachel Davidson to a Conus shell, contradictory and impenetrable. Rachel battled for independence, torn by her need for Taylor's embraces and her impassioned desire to be her own woman. Could they both succumb to the temptation of the tropi-

cal paradise and still be true to their hearts?

#9 DECEMBER 32nd . . . AND ALWAYS

By Marie Michael
Blaise Hamilton made her feel like the most desirable woman on earth. Pat opened herself to emotions she'd thought buried with her late husband. Together they were unbeatable as they worked to build the jet of her late husband's dreams. Time seemed to be running out and yet—would ALWAYS be long enough?

#10 HARD DRIVIN' MAN

By Nancy Carlson
Sabrina sensed Jacy in hot pursuit, as she maneuvered her truck around the racetrack, and recalled his arms clasping her to him. Was he only using her feelings so he could take over her trucking company? Their passion knew no limits as they raced full speed toward love.

#11 BELOVED INTRUDER

By Noelle Berry McCue
Shannon Douglas hated

Michael Brady from the moment he brought the breezes of life into her shadowy existence. Yet a specter of the past remained to torment her and threaten their future. Could he subdue the demons that haunted her, and carry her to true happiness?

#12 HUNTER'S PAYNE
By Joan J. Domning
P. Lee Payne strode into Karen Hunter's office demanding to know why she was stalking him. She was determined to interview the mysterious photographer. She uncovered his concealed emotions, but could the secrets their hearts confided protect their love, or would harsh daylight shatter their fragile alliance?

#13 TIGER LADY
By Joan J. Domning
Who *was* this mysterious lover she'd never seen who courted her on the office computer, and nicknamed her Tiger Lady? And could he compete with Larry Hart, who came to repair the computer

and stayed to short-circuit her emotions? How could she choose between poetry and passion—between soul and Hart?

#14 STORMY VOWS
By Iris Johansen
Independent Brenna Sloan wasn't strong enough to reach out for the love she needed, and Michael Donovan knew only how to take—until he met Brenna. Only after a misunderstanding nearly destroyed their happiness, did they surrender to their fiery passion.

#15 BRIEF DELIGHT
By Helen Mittermeyer
Darius Chadwick felt his chest tighten with desire as Cygnet Melton glided into his life. But a prelude was all they knew before Cyg fled in despair, certain she had shattered the dream they had made together. Their hearts had collided in an instant; now could they seize the joy of enduring love?

#16 A VERY RELUCTANT KNIGHT
By Billie Green
A tornado brought them together in a storm cel-

lar. But Maggie Sims and Mark Wilding were anything but perfectly matched. Maggie wanted to prove he was wrong about her. She knew they didn't belong together, but when he caressed her, she was swept up in a passion that promised a lifetime of love.

#17 TEMPEST AT SEA
By Iris Johansen
Jane Smith sneaked aboard playboy-director Jake Dominic's yacht on a dare. The muscled arms that captured her were inescapable—and suddenly Jane found herself agreeing to a month-long cruise of the Caribbean. Jane had never given much thought to love, but under Jake's tutelage she discovered its magic . . . and its torment.

#18 AUTUMN FLAMES
By Sara Orwig
Lily Dunbar had ventured too far into the wilderness of Reece Wakefield's vast Chilean ranch; now an oncoming storm thrust her into his arms . . . and he refused to let her go. Could he lure her, step by seductive step, away from the life she had forged for herself, to find her real home in his arms?

#19 PFARR LAKE AFFAIR
By Joan J. Domning
Leslie Pfarr hadn't been back at her father's resort for an hour before she was pitched into the lake by Eric Nordstrom! The brash teenager who'd made her childhood a constant torment had grown into a handsome man. But when he began persuading her to fall in love, Leslie wondered if she was courting disaster.

#20 HEART ON A STRING
By Carla Neggers
One look at heart surgeon Paul Houghton Welling told JoAnna Radcliff he belonged in the stuffy society world she'd escaped for a cottage in Pigeon Cove. She firmly believed she'd never fit into his life, but he set out to show her she was wrong. She was the puppet master, but he knew how to keep her heart on a string.

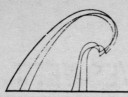

LOVESWEPT

Love Stories you'll never forget by authors you'll always remember

Prices and availability subject to change without notice.

Buy them at your local bookstore or use this handy coupon for ordering:

Bantam Books, Inc., Dept. SW, 414 East Golf Road, Des Plaines, Ill. 60016

Please send me the books I have checked above. I am enclosing
$_____ (please add $1.25 to cover postage and handling). Send
check or money order—no cash or C.O.D.'s please.

Mr/Ms_____

Address_____

City/State_____ Zip_____

SW—9/84

Please allow four to six weeks for delivery. This offer expires 3/85.

LOVESWEPT

Love Stories you'll never forget by authors you'll always remember

☐	21630	Lightning That Lingers #25 Sharon & Tom Curtis	$1.95
☐	21631	Once In a Blue Moon #26 Billie J. Green	$1.95
☐	21632	The Bronzed Hawk #27 Iris Johansen	$1.95
☐	21637	Love, Catch a Wild Bird #28 Anne Reisser	$1.95
☐	21626	The Lady and the Unicorn #29 Iris Johansen	$1.95
☐	21628	Winner Take All #30 Nancy Holder	$1.95
☐	21635	The Golden Valkyrie #31 Iris Johansen	$1.95
☐	21638	C.J.'s Fate #32 Kay Hooper	$1.95
☐	21639	The Planting Season #33 Dorothy Garlock	$1.95
☐	21629	For Love of Sami #34 Fayrene Preston	$1.95
☐	21627	The Trustworthy Redhead #35 Iris Johansen	$1.95
☐	21636	A Touch of Magic #36 Carla Neggers	$1.95
☐	21641	Irresistible Forces #37 Marie Michael	$1.95
☐	21642	Temporary Forces #38 Billie Green	$1.95
☐	21646	Kirsten's Inheritance #39 Joan Domning	$2.25
☐	21645	Return to Santa Flores #40 Iris Johansen	$2.25
☐	21656	The Sophisticated Mountain Gal #41 Joan Bramsch	$2.25
☐	21655	Heat Wave #42 Sara Orwig	$2.25
☐	21649	To See the Daisies . . . First #43 Billie Green	$2.25
☐	21648	No Red Roses #44 Iris Johansen	$2.25
☐	21644	That Old Feeling #45 Fayrene Preston	$2.25
☐	21650	Something Different #46 Kay Hooper	$2.25

Prices and availability subject to change without notice.

Buy them at your local bookstore or use this handy coupon for ordering: